FAULTS IN FATE
A Vein Chronicles Novella

ANNE MALCOM

Copyright © 2018 by Anne Malcom

All rights reserved.

No part of this book may be reproduced in any form or by any electronic or mechanical means, including information storage and retrieval systems, without written permission from the author, except for the use of brief quotations in a book review.

Cover Design: Simply Defined Art
Editing: Hot Tree Editing

To everyone who believes in magic.

The Four

Witches are born of the earth, from the soul of nature itself. No god bestowed power over the first mortal women to gain the powers of the elements... no, it was the benevolent power of nature herself that gifted the first of our kind with their magic.

"It was neither good nor evil what The Four were blessed with, just power itself. But it is dangerous, that neutrality, especially when put into human spirits. It is forbidden to use natural powers to create unnatural acts. This crime is unforgivable. Any child of the earth who choses darkness over the spirit of The Four is lost forever."

Chapter One

A *witch*. The mere thought was toxic in his mind.

All these years—all these *centuries*—he'd been waiting for the female who would belong to him. Who the gods and the animal inside him had tied to him, the one thing he might be able to hold onto in the world that had abandoned him. His destiny. And she was a fucking *witch*.

He'd despised the supernatural world ever since he had escaped decades of torture. Shunned the pack that had failed him—that he had failed. The failure resulted in pain that stalked after him, somehow one step behind him and ahead of him at the same time.

He despised every creature on the planet, even of his own race, but he did not despise *her*.

It was biologically impossible for a wolf to hate his one true mate. The animal inside him and the ancient instinct rendered such a thing impossible.

He despised the fact that she was a witch.

One that, from what he could see, only had one companion, a *vampire*.

And she was a mercenary, not doing good for free but doing anything—good or evil—as long as she got paid.

Not that he cared about good or evil, but fuck, he'd expected his mate to be better than him, of his own species. He'd needed it. Wolves were not designed to be alone. They needed their pack. They needed other animals to run to when in their truest of forms, especially on the full moon. Every time he changed there was unnatural agony in the solitude that surrounded him.

But he was used to pain, so he endured.

That was his existence. Enduring.

Until her.

And she was more pain than anything he'd experienced.

His mate.

The witch.

He craved her the second his eyes touched her shapely body with its unusual and strangely erotic markings covering it. Until that moment, he'd hated the way humans had repeatedly marked and altered their bodies with insipid scribblings.

Hers, he wanted to explore every single one. Touch them. Run his tongue along them.

The animal inside him demanded he take her. Claim her as his the moment he glimpsed her in the rotten bar where he spent his nights, waiting, plotting.

But the man in him knew better. She was not of his kind, and she would not recognize their fate as a shewolf would've.

It infuriated him.

She did.

The way she showed her flesh like some kind of wanton woman. Her dirty mouth. The way she played with her mortality as if she wasn't the only being in the supernatural community who had it. He knew little about witches, but he knew even though they had the ability to live forever, they didn't have the healing capacity of most immortals and that meant they were as close to mortal as they ever could be. It was their magic that protected them.

The only one who could die, almost as easily as a human welcomed the abyss.

The thought of her succumbing to it when he'd only just found her filled him with dread so heavy he could barely walk with it.

But he did walk with it. Every one of his steps ghosted hers.

He tore down the foe that she seemed to face off with every night, the danger she danced with, the death she flirted with. He tore out the throats of those who threatened her, but did not touch her, grasp her and never let go.

He'd steal into the shadows.

Watching.

Waiting.

The wolf didn't like waiting.

It hated it, rattling inside the cage in fury.

But he knew he had to. His instinct, honed over centuries told him he must. So with great struggle, he did.

He would claim his mate.

Or he would die trying.

🐾

"YOU WILL DIE FOR THAT, BITCH," the demon snarled, speaking about the flaming remains of what used to be his best friend.

His best friend who enjoyed torturing and killing humans before he yanked their souls from their broken bodies.

So not cool.

But not the reason for the smoke that would stick to Sophie's hair for days, no matter how many times she washed it.

No, she was getting paid for this particular bonfire. She didn't do assassinations much—that was more her vampire buddy Duncan's thing—but she dabbled when she had a free Tuesday.

Her palms crackled as the demon approached. "*Witch* bitch, thank you very much," she corrected, grinning as the demon's eyes turned black, as they did right before the whole soul-sucking thing. "And it ain't my death that Hades is gonna get giddy about. I'm afraid it's yours. Say hey to your daddy for me." The power building in her palms itched to be released, to kill, its hunger for death more unyielding every time Sophie met the grave.

One of the many reasons not to die.

Before she could barbeque the demon á la well done, a shape tore through the alley, barely visible even with Sophie's improved sight. Not as good as a vampire's but much better than that of a lowly human.

Growling and the tearing of flesh emanated from where the demon had been moments before, and then there was silence, death chased away all sound. She was used to the void it created, but it didn't mean that goose bumps didn't rise on every exposed piece of Sophie's skin.

Another blur, a scent, a strange jump in Sophie's stomach as she sensed... something. An instinct long forgotten, one that yanked at her psyche with the presence of an immortal being that had torn the demon's throat out and left the alley with dizzying speed before Sophie could even char the edges of his flesh for taking her kill.

Werewolf.

She readied herself to catch onto the fast-dissipating aura hanging amidst the death in the alley so she could imprint it and then do a scrying spell. Without it, she wouldn't have a hope in heaven to find whoever—or, more aptly, *whatever*—she was going to give a lecture to about demon killing etiquette.

"Dude, you killed demons without me. That is *such* a shitty friend move."

A vampire with bloodred hair, a great winged eyeliner and a

kickass pair of Manolos appeared in front of her, pouting like a teenager.

Her best friend, Isla Rominskitoff, was almost five hundred years old in immortal years, though her maturity was closer to that of a sixteen-year-old. Precisely why she was her bestie.

That and they had the same shoe size and liked killing things and causing general mayhem.

Isla's appearance was usually welcomed, but it jolted her out of her concentration enough for her to lose grip on the aura and therefore the opportunity to track the being it belonged to.

Why was it such a big deal to her anyway?

She scowled at Isla, irritated at her best friend for the first time in decades. Other people got irritated with them, they did not irritate each other.

Well, except when Isla almost tricked Sophie into marrying Henry VIII. That was a dick move.

"Well, if you were a little more punctual and answered your phone once in a while, you might've gotten in on this," Sophie replied, nodding to the charred ashes and the throatless demon. She noted the black blood trickling from the head that was still attached. "I even left you the best part, decapitation. And you say I'm a bad friend."

Isla looked over her shoulder, grinning as her fangs extended. In a blink of a human eye—Sophie was able to follow her movements, unlike the wolf of before—she was standing outside the pool of blood, thinking of her shoes, obviously. She bent down, grasping the horns of the demon as he reverted from his human form.

She glanced at the tear in his throat, then eyed Sophie with a raised brow. "Since when do you kill by mauling?" she asked with suspicion. "Do you have a taste for demon flesh now? It's okay, you can tell me. I'll only tease you mercilessly for a hundred years or so."

Sophie scowled at her. "I'm just testing out new spells," she lied. The words were out of her mouth before she'd even had a chance to think on them. That wasn't unusual on principle, but Sophie never lied to Isla. Except when she'd asked her if it was possible to get magical calf implants, but that was for good reason.

Why did she want to keep the presence of some unknown werewolf a secret?

There was the wet gurgling of blood, then the tearing of flesh that chased away most of Sophie's thoughts. Isla stepped back, tossing the head over her shoulder.

She glanced down to frown at the single droplet of blood that was staining her white boob tube; somehow she'd managed to get nothing on the high-waisted white pants that were tailored to her slim body. Who said vampires wore black lace and velvet? Isla had a violent dislike for the fabric.

She glared at Sophie. Isla felt very strongly about bloodstains getting on her clothes, but refused to wear things that would be a little more suitable considering she had to spill blood on the daily to survive.

"I'm not letting the fact that I have to tear people's throats out and drink their blood hinder my fashion choices. It would be immoral," she'd snapped the last time Sophie mentioned it.

"I'm thinking a no for this spell," she hissed, stepping over the body as she tapped a button on her phone. "Too fucking messy."

Sophie fell into step with her as they exited the dingy alley and rejoined the masses rushing down the New York street, unaware they were a handful of feet away from a witch and a vampire who'd just killed two demons.

"Yeah, I need a cleanup on 7th and Madison," Isla said into her phone. Listening to the excited squawk on the other end of the phone, she pinched the bridge of her nose. "Yes, Scott, it's me, undead and fabulous. But I'm busy, so just get the cleanup done and stop saying the word 'sidekick' or I'll eviscerate you and your entire Vein Line, mmmkay? Buh-bye."

She shoved her phone back in her Chanel, rolling her eyes at Sophie.

"You're buying me a new top," she said. "Then we're getting absolutely trashed and cursing every human we see smoking an E-cig."

Sophie shook her head with a grin, preparing for just another night with her bestie, trying to force her reaction to the wolf's presence from her mind.

Easier said than done.

※

INSTANCES like the one in the alley became frighteningly common for Sophie.

Every time she was on a job—or, more often lately, hunting down hybrid vampires, turned from humans using dark magic—she'd felt a presence. Not malice... toward her, at least. It was toward any being she faced off with.

She did her best to snatch at the dissipating plumes of his aura—she knew it was a he, the feeling of his presence overwhelmingly male—but she always got distracted by a snapping hybrid or a testy vampire before she could get a grip on it.

The first time she'd really *seen* him was in a crowded human nightclub. She was the only supernatural at that particular loud, sweaty, tacky establishment serving overpriced drinks and playing bad music.

She'd designed it that way.

It was her secret shame. Pretending to belong among the throngs of idiotic humans whose lives were fleeting and simple. She'd pretend that her life was simple and that her biggest problem was a bad hair day, a bad molly, or a guy who just wasn't that into her.

Pretending because she never had bad hair days—though Isla would disagree with her there—she didn't need drugs to be awesome, and every guy, demon, and vampire was *always* into her. And a particular human slayer named Silver who just wouldn't accept his new place in the friend zone. A place she'd put the sexy surfer dude in the second she'd tasted the wolf's presence in the alley that day.

Her life was awesome. She wouldn't change it for the world—or the end of the world. But things were becoming too real lately, things like finding out that Isla had been spelled to become mortal and eventually die by the witches they'd been battling and still didn't know how to defeat. Sophie didn't even know how to counter the spell.

Scratch that, she did find out how to fight a death spell. With more death. More accurately, Isla drinking her slayer boyfriend's blood—which had the pesky side effect of instant death.

She had yet to tell Isla. Not because Isla would lose it. She likely wouldn't even blink. Nothing worried her.

Nothing bothered Sophie usually. But this held a finality to it that somehow Sophie was certain would be death.

And she felt helpless, angry, wanting to level the entire city with her power.

So she came to the place that might quell the need to become inhuman.

Sometimes she just needed to be a simple human with simple problems, pretend she didn't have something inside her that scared her so bad she sometimes wished for the one thing immortals despised—humanity.

That was what gave him away. That and the werewolf stench.

The lack of humanity.

And the fact he was focused solely on her. He wasn't there to hunt, like many of the supernatural community did. No, it almost seemed he was there for *her*.

She'd locked eyes with him across the dance floor. And it wasn't like those idiotic movie moments when the crowd slowed down and blurred away and the music muted.

The bass was still so loud it made her teeth chatter, sweaty inebriated humans still shoved at her and hit on her, and the world still moved. As it always did.

But eyes that seemed to glow gold and see into her fucked-up soul stilled her.

For a hot minute, at least.

Then she quickly looked away and resumed dancing, pretending the large, muscled, scruffy, and sinfully wild wolf hadn't just been undressing her soul with his eyes.

※

SHE'D PURPOSEFULLY WALKED down a deserted alley an hour later.

It's exactly what the victim did in every movie.

Scantily clad, helpless, and ultimately dead.

Sophie was scantily clad, in a bloodred dress with safety pins holding the sides together, and matching thigh-high boots that every hooker would die to possess.

But she wasn't helpless, and wasn't looking to die that night.

She was trying to lure a wolf, and was dressed for it, wearing red and everything, even if she didn't have the hood.

"I'm not going to grandma's house, and I'm sorry to inform you that your teeth aren't abnormally large, considering the company I keep, and they're not going to be used for eating me." She turned, regarding the man who had followed her into the depths of the alley. "In *any* sense of the word," she finished with a raised brow. Hot excitement shot through her belly at the mere thought of this man, this wolf, *eating her.*

He didn't reply. Not a single word.

With his mouth, at least.

It seemed these intense immortals with their equally penetrating and alpha gazes were becoming all too common in Sophie's life. It was bad enough to see Isla have to weather such stares coming from a slayer who should've wanted her fangs as a necklace, and the king of all fangers who should've executed her for insolence decades before.

But she was now getting treated to her very own soulful gaze.

From a *werewolf,* of all things.

An *attractive* werewolf at that.

She'd forced herself not to linger on him at the club, and it was hard. Some ancient and carnal part of her demanded she not only rove her eyes over him but get closer to, touch, and taste him. The need had been overwhelming, and it snaked around her motor skills even now, in some brutal marriage with that ancient power creeping through her bloodstream, trying to gain hold.

She fought both needs.

Even though she wasn't going to let herself touch, there wasn't any harm in looking, was there? She'd give herself a quick perv, then blast him with a medium punch of power and get the heck out of Dodge.

Maybe look up a demon from her little pink book to scratch the itch she hadn't even known existed until just over an hour before.

Demons were usually her go-to. Warlocks were underneath them, though it was strictly orgasm then bail, because warlocks didn't like being with more powerful witches. They had a total complex, and Sophie may have technically had an eternity on this earth—if she could hold on to at least one life—but she didn't have time for that.

Humans in a pinch, though then she'd have to expend energy

erasing their memories because she had no control of her powers during sex—and humans couldn't really miss the rush of magic expelling from every part of her body and shocking them with a low burst of power that more often than not rendered them unconscious.

They just weren't strong enough.

She didn't go near vampires. *Eww.* Despite how drop-dead hot they were, they were also drop-dead *evil.*

Isla and Scott were exceptions. Well, Isla was the exception because Sophie didn't swing that way, and Scott was more like a goofy brother with fangs than anything else.

Though she'd toyed with tangling with evil when she'd laid eyes on the vampire king, even if he'd only had eyes for Isla.

But no wolves.

Ever.

She found their lack of control distasteful, plus they were animalistic, alpha, and only one step above Neanderthal.

She'd imagined their version of sex as rutting a female, grunting brutally before reaching release and prowling off.

No thank you.

But this wolf was changing something. Taking away the thoughts of dirty, animalistic sex.

No, he wasn't taking that away. He was making her *want* it.

Not her, Sophie, but this new urge inside her that she didn't recognize.

This was becoming a frightful norm, meeting new and dangerous parts of herself that had been lingering in the depths of her mind.

And this new being *liked* the wolf.

He was wild. From his shoulder-length midnight hair to the rough smattering of stubble—bordering on a beard—covering his strong jaw. His brows were strong yet somehow groomed, framing creamy caramel eyes that glowed gold in the dim light of 3:00 a.m.

His clothes were worn but clean and good quality. His tan leather jacket could barely encase his huge muscled form.

He must've had to scour Men's Big and Tall for that.

He had on a black henley underneath that clung to his concrete abs, the outline visible thanks to her improved eyesight. That spell had been worth the days of recovery afterward for this moment alone.

His jeans were black too, faded at the thigh and molded over his legs that could have doubled as tree trucks.

She swallowed roughly as she moved back to his eyes. He'd clearly been doing the same thing with her. And in the short time it had taken her to rake her gaze back up, his eyes glowed brighter, like dim torches sprouting out from his brain.

Creepy.

Though she guessed she couldn't really talk about creepy considering she barely recognized herself in the mirror these days.

He was six feet from her, and that seemed too far and yet too close. Her instincts screamed at her to run and also stay at the same time.

She never ran.

Not even when it got her killed.

He hadn't seemed content in their unhurried perusal of each other, nor in the silence, despite the fact he had yet to speak. He radiated a wild, almost feral desperation; it seeped from his pores, saturating the aura that pulsated black and golds.

All witches had the ability to read auras, to a point. The more connection they had to their psychic skill, the more apt they were at reading energy. An aura was just that, a field of energy wrapped tight around a person, spilling out into the air around them. The stronger the being was, the further the aura stretched.

The wolf's aura licked at the tops of her boots.

There was danger to it. But somehow not directed at her.

Bodily, at least.

What she sensed in him made her wish he meant her bodily harm. *That* she could deal with.

The second he lost control with the beast clawing at his irises and stepped his booted foot forward, Sophie called forth the magic that had been lingering beneath her skin. It crept into the air, surrounded her, pulsed within her spirit, and her hands crackled with blue light.

She didn't unleash it on him, not yet.

"I wouldn't if I were you," she warned, her voice thick.

She struggled to keep it familiar, to hold on to herself. Lately every time she used magic, even for the simplest of things—like killing a demon, or cursing people who cut in front of her at Starbucks—she lacked the purchase on it she had before. The ancient power that had slowly been clawing its way up her soul gained purchase with every spell she cast.

It seduced her with the sheer amount of power she'd command if only she just welcomed it in. Her bones seemed cold, empty, and if she let it, she could fill them, warm them with a power no witch had known. It was intoxicating, the knowledge that she had access to such power.

But there was no control in it. Sophie knew that the second she started spouting prophecies and journeying back to nineteenth-century England.

Control was one of the most important things in witchcraft. Without it, the ancient art, the magic coming from the earth itself, would consume the witch. Clutch her and then yank her back into the core, claiming her vessel for its own until there was nothing left of her but an empty shell.

Sophie was so not hot on being an empty shell, not with her kickass personality. Hence her fighting against the power.

The wolf stopped, thankfully, which meant she didn't have to zap him with the power leaking from her palms. Though she had to actively stop herself.

It yearned to be used. To destroy him, even though part of her was sickened at the thought of it.

His glowing eyes fixated on her palms, on the very air around her, as if he could see the way the particles bent to her will. If she so wished, she could suck all the oxygen out of this alley so he could no longer breathe. She could drop the temperature so his blood froze in his veins, or make it boil at the same heat as the surface of the sun.

She didn't do that, of course. And she'd been very careful to hide that nifty little power. Control over the elements was awesome when she'd forgotten to wear a jacket and it was chilly. Not so awesome if her coven found out and had her sequestered.

She eyed the wolf, the power rolling through her sharpening her vision. "What do you want?" she demanded.

He wanted something, that was for sure. A werewolf didn't follow a witch into a dark alley for no reason—no matter how hot her outfit was.

His mouth remained closed.

His eyes did not, swirling through the magic, battling at it to entice her with something more dangerous than the complete destruction that power promised.

Something much worse than that.

Something that would leave her as an empty shell, if she let it.

Sophie wasn't about to let anything—or anyone—take away who she was.

She hit him with a warning shot, nothing more than a slap in the face really. He flinched only slightly and his jaw hardened, anger seeping from every part of him. His fists clenched at his sides, claws pushing from his fingertips.

But he did not move.

Did not attack.

"I know wolves aren't known for their intelligence, but they do have control over their vocal chords," Sophie gritted out against the magic that was urging her forward.

More, it demanded.

She ignored it.

"So I repeat my question—what do you want?" she bit out, trying for the casual tone that was her norm, despite the overarching need to release every inch of power stretching at her skin.

End him. End this entire city. Bend it to your will.

His jaw flexed, eyes somehow both swirling yet unmoving.

The low growl of his beast echoed in the alley.

And somehow that growl worked as an anchor to keep Sophie in the moment, to stop her from succumbing to the power that had never felt so intoxicating and toxic at the same time.

In the midst of this, she'd lost purchase on the situation that she'd been so sure she'd held ironclad control over, because he was right there, right up in her grill.

His eyes radiated warmth, like she was in front of an open fire, every part of his body thrumming with dark energy even the being inside her couldn't compete with. Her power was wild, but one day it might be tamed. His power was different. His was a beast, and it could never be tamed.

He wasn't touching her, but every inch of her skin was tattooed with his presence in a way she despised and loved simultaneously.

"Everything," he growled, voice guttural and rough, as if he wasn't used to forming words. "I want everything from you."

In the one long blink that it took her to process those words, the alley was empty. Only the heat in the air and the rapid beat of her heart signified the wolf had been there.

She glared at the mouth of the alley, then upward, seeing the dark shadow of his form against the crescent moon before he disappeared onto a rooftop.

She scowled, forcing the power from her hands to retreat back inside her. "Fucking wolves," she muttered, striding out toward the sidewalk, intent on pretending that had never happened.

※

SHE'D KNOWN it had been too easy in the alley.

Much too easy.

But she hoped, with all the things going on lately, that maybe she deserved a little easy and had deluded herself into thinking the wolf would be nothing but a memory by the time she returned home.

Not only had she not been able to stop thinking about those golden eyes on the forty-block walk she'd made herself take—in six-inch heels, no less—but she'd found herself having to actively stop herself from doing a scrying spell for him. She didn't just have snatches of his aura now; it stuck to every part of her skin, burrowing under it.

It was crazy. She was desperate to be in his presence though she'd only spent a handful of minutes in it that very night.

Yeah, he was hot as all sin, but he was a *werewolf.*

And he had that intense look like Thorne and Rick. The one that spelled destruction for a once independent and kickass female. Not that Isla wasn't kickass still, but she had a weakness now—love.

And Sophie knew this wasn't love because she wasn't an idiot and she hadn't even given him a BJ—*that* was the true sign of love. She decided it was infatuation coupled with sexual frustration.

That's at least what she'd told herself until she stepped over the magical threshold to her apartment building and sensed the tears in her magical locks.

No one should've gotten through them.

Even the strongest of witches.

But there he was, standing in the middle of her foyer, dripping his sexiness and intensity all over the place.

His eyes burned into her.

She froze.

Even her magic froze.

Ordinarily on encountering an intruder in her sacred space—her awesome loft in Soho—she would kill them immediately with a burst of power that would chop their heads off.

The werewolf's scruffy and sexy head stayed attached to his wide and muscled shoulders.

"You need to leave," she gritted through her teeth. "If you want to live to see another full moon, with all of your paws intact, you will leave the way you came and make sure our paths never cross again."

He didn't move. Didn't even flinch, as if the room didn't pulsate with magic that she knew he would sense. All immortals sensed magic. It was what fueled them, after all. A healthy dose of biology, of course, but you couldn't believe that vampires lived on blood, almost invincible, that demons clawed themselves up from the bowels of the earth, that men could turn into wolves, without a little magic.

Or a lot of it.

Witches themselves were made of a fuck of a lot more of it than most immortals. And unlike other immortals, it didn't come from gods, their power. It came from the earth, the natural world that always had magic since the dawn of time, but only the descendants of The Four could wield it. It was passed down through the maternal line, mother to daughter.

"Wolf," she hissed, her palms itching. "You're playing with fire."

She wasn't lying. Her power was quickly recovering from whatever about the wolf's appearance had stuttered it.

She didn't have the time to inspect the thought that *nothing* had paused her power in the century and a half she'd had it.

She didn't have time because the wolf was across the room and in front of her before any more rational thought could run through her head. Not that much rational thought ran through Sophie's head on any given day.

He wasn't just in front of her—the wolf was *kissing* her.

She didn't even fight it.

At first because she was shocked.

Sophie didn't do shocked. She was unflappable. And she read people's auras well, so she usually knew what was coming in any given interaction.

But she hadn't seen *this* coming.

Which was why the wolf still had his legs to stand on and lips to kiss her with.

He growled at the back of his throat when she melted against him, automatically kissing him back, fighting at the tongue that was plundering her mouth.

Damn you, autokiss!

His hand was running through her hair, yanking at the strands while his other pulled at her hip, bringing her body into his rock-hard torso.

Their contact, even over top of clothes—his, because she wasn't wearing that many—worked like an electric shock to her system.

She didn't think of anything other than *more*.

Apparently he was thinking the same thing, because she was in his arms with her legs around his hips and her panties pressing into his length encased in denim before she could say friction.

She moaned in his mouth as his rapid movements toward her bed pushed his cock harder against the lace that covered her core. The sensitivity of that area was somehow barely bearable, with that contact alone almost bringing her to climax.

The air roared around them like she'd left all the windows open in the middle of a hurricane.

All the windows were closed, and there weren't any hurricanes in New York.

It was her. She was the hurricane. It was them, more precisely what they were doing, that was causing the change in atmosphere in her apartment.

Another growl as he threw her against the bed so hard the legs collapsed and her body jolted as the frame hit wooden floors.

She barely noticed.

Nor did she feel the glass that landed on her body as the windows shattered with the force of her power.

All she felt was the heat radiating from the wolf in front of her, leaking from the eyes that had changed shape, slanted, widened, like those of an animal. His form shimmered for just a moment as the wolf inside him battled for power.

Sophie watched it, a thin sheen of sweat settling over her body with anticipation. It didn't scare her, that battle between wolf and man in front of her—the battle to claim her body. No, it *excited* her, sending sparks of pleasure through her entire body. Her nipples strained against the thin fabric encasing them, almost painful with her need for him. Her panties dampened as she ached to have him in her most sacred spot.

He growled again, his nostrils flaring as if he scented the way her arousal penetrated the magic-filled air. His hands became claws and he used them to rip at his clothes, tearing at them until he stood in front of her, gloriously naked, chest heaving.

She didn't even have time to appreciate the sheer male glory of his physique, marble marred with vicious scars that made him more dangerous and delicious simultaneously.

She didn't have time to think about what an utter idiot she was for marveling at a male wolf.

No, because the male wolf in question moved in a blur and his claws cut through all the fabric of her clubbing clothes until they were even smaller pieces of fabric than they originally were.

Her underwear fared the same.

His golden gaze went to her boots, and even in her near madness, she hoped he wouldn't put his claws to those too. They were worth two thousand dollars and her favorite pair. Even her best enchantments likely wouldn't save them if a werewolf's claws took to them.

But he left them, surely not for the same reasons as her, but she was relieved nonetheless.

Then she wasn't relieved because she was damn near insane with ecstasy. His mouth settled between her legs in yet another blur, no warming up, no teasing, nothing. He was just *there*.

Her nails tore into her comforter, and blue shafts of light erupted from the skin of her forearms, singeing the curtains.

She didn't even notice, nor think about the potential fire hazard.

No, her mind was on the werewolf's mouth, lapping at her, devouring her in a way that was both brutally wild and somehow infuriatingly gentle.

"Wolf," she screamed. "I'm gonna—"

She was cut off by his guttural growl. The vibrations against her sensitive skin tipped her over the edge, and the room spun and exploded at the same time as a tidal wave of pleasure ruined her.

Her bones were dust.

Skin scorched.

Heartbeat cracking at her ribs.

And he *wasn't done*.

His mouth was at her nipples, suckling on the aching nubs. Shoots of pleasure made her body twitch, and then pain mingled with it as he sank his now elongated teeth into her skin. It melted for him like butter.

She didn't even care. She *liked* that he was drawing her blood, tearing at her flesh. Some wild part of her craved it.

Her lead arms managed to lift themselves, her palms crackling with magic as she tore her hands through his hair, yanking at his strands in much the same way he had with her a lifetime ago. Though she didn't have his strength, she had the command of her powers to seep her own release into his skin, share her pleasure.

She'd never done such a thing before, never wanted to do such a thing—her pleasure was hers alone. If dudes got their end away, then that was all gravy; otherwise, she didn't care. But now it was little more than second nature.

His entire form froze, something she would've sworn wouldn't have been possible before, when his body was in the grips of the beast.

But everything she'd believed about... well, everything was being pushed away like dust in the breeze. Or more accurately like a barn in a tornado.

He was tearing through it all, but she didn't care because it was fucking *awesome*.

Golden irises met hers, the man and the beast both stilling as she poured yet more of her pleasure into his body. He grunted at the release she was sharing with him, his body taut, everything marble.

Something akin to wonder, adoration even, passed over his face.

But no, that wasn't possible. That couldn't be possible. That would be the only thing possible to extinguish the flames licking at every part of her body. There was no place for tenderness here, there couldn't be. Tenderness gave way to feelings, to something Sophie had vowed off.

"Witch," he growled, his voice liquid.

She immediately stopped the flow of magic and he twitched, his eyes hardening and narrowing.

She yanked harder at his hair, tearing at it with force she knew garnered pain, even in a wolf. Her magic made sure of that.

He didn't move, didn't even cry out, but that wildness returned.

"Fuck me, wolf," she demanded, voice horse.

He didn't need to be told twice, up and at her entrance in little more than a moment. There was no pause, no gentle stroking of her head that she feared he might do. No, he didn't even wait to ask if she was ready, just plunged inside her.

They both cried out at his perfectly brutal entrance.

More windows shattered throughout the apartment.

The wind resumed again.

It was all inconsequential.

Her fingernails sank into the skin of his back, drawing blood. She didn't even think of it as she let his lifeblood sink into her skin, feed into her magic. He growled at the contact—surely not the magic, as he wouldn't have noted it—and then he moved.

Fuck, did he *move*.

His body pounded into her with a ferocity that would've broken a mortal woman. Shit, it almost broke *her*, and she was a lot more durable than the original model.

But it didn't.

It took her to the brink of destruction, of pain, to the abyss that she'd become so familiar with, then tore her right back.

Every inch of her body was fire, even the parts she'd been so certain would be chilled from the grave forever.

Everything was an inferno.

His mouth attached against hers, teeth sinking into her lip, drawing more blood, sucking it into his own.

She didn't even blink at that, simply reveled in it. She'd absorbed his blood mere moments—or was it hours?—before. Turnabout was fair play. And the moment he swallowed her blood —not for nourishment, like a leech, but for something else—a climax raked over her, shuddering her delicate bones, shaking her very core.

He growled as his form shimmered once more while she clenched against his cock, urging his own release. Hands—no, claws circled at her neck. They could've easily snapped it, scored the skin, severed an artery. And she'd be bye-bye immortal. She wouldn't have even been able to defend herself in the midst of the most earth-shaking orgasm of her life.

And she didn't care. There were worse ways to go. She'd experienced them.

But she stayed alive, because she knew this heaven didn't exist in the afterlife.

Dim pain erupted in her shoulder as he cracked her collarbone and roared out his release, pumping himself into her with such wild abandon that it pushed her right over the edge again.

The abyss welcomed her that time, wrapping around her consciousness in its seductive embrace.

She thought she'd heard him yell something in the moments before her pleasure became too much to handle.

But she couldn't have.

It was impossible.

⁑

"Mine!" he roared, both in his human voice and his beast's. Both beings within him recognized her for what she was.

His mate.

His fated one.

The woman he was tied to, who he had claim over, for the rest of his life.

For the rest of forever.

The one he would kill for, die for, and more importantly *live* for.

Expelling his seed into his woman's sweet and tight velvet was hands down the best experience of his long life.

Not that there was much to compare it to.

But it was something so sweet, so heavenly, it had no equal.

And it would have no equal. He would be claiming her, fucking her, every moment he could until time ended.

It took him long and ecstatic moments to gain agency over his own body, to grasp true lucidity once more.

He had collapsed onto her tiny body in the midst of his release, aching to have every inch of their naked skin touching his. The wolf inside of him required skin-to-skin contact one of the most important things to his species. Other than being inside one's mate.

But his human side wanted her sweet and smooth skin against his, rough and brutal. The need had been so desperate he'd forgotten his own strength, his own weight, and collapsed all of it onto her.

On that realization, panic took over pleasure and he immediately lifted his body from hers, ignoring the roar of his beast.

She was limp, her eyelids fluttered closed, her pale skin flushed at her face. But it was not his warmth that had discolored the rest of her body.

Ice sank into his heart and he let out a brutal curse as his horrified gaze ran over the purple and black skin of her entire body.

His stomach roiled.

He smelled the broken bones in her ribs, in her collarbone, the pain she would feel once waking.

Waking.

He'd rendered her unconscious.

He'd battered and broken the one true being that belonged to him while he was too lost in his own pleasure.

"Gods, what have I done?" he uttered.

Chapter Two

Minutes were little more than nothing in an immortal's life. Less than nothing when decades passed like hours.

But the twelve minutes that had passed since she'd surrendered to the darkness were longer than the eight centuries he'd spent on this earth.

He paced the ruined apartment, barely seeing the broken glass that crunched under his bare feet. Or the ruined furniture. Or the singed curtain, though he smelled the burn and vaguely wondered if his witch had caused it.

Of course she'd caused it. That was her power. Even now he sensed it in the air, blanketing everything around them.

It had been how he found her in that pulsating mess of humans weeks before. He'd been blocks away, hunting a pack of vampires that was stalking young women.

He'd abandoned the doomed women without even a second thought the moment he'd caught a whiff of her power.

Scenting things was hard in this cesspit of a city, full of trash and humans and filth. He was a good tracker, the best in fact, but even he found it difficult to scent someone more than three blocks away.

Not her.

He would've scented her from the other side of the country.

Or so it had seemed at that moment.

He wasn't even sure if it was his mate's scent or her all-encompassing power that drew him. The beast inside of him had basic intrinsic survival instincts. And it had sensed a threat. A big one. One of the biggest he'd ever faced.

Inside his mate.

The fact had worried him slightly, though not as much as it should've since his elation at finally finding her blew everything else away.

Now he praised the gods for whatever this power was. Because it was able to repair her quickly. Quicker than normal.

On another glance to the bed, he was confronted with bruises. Had they changed in color? He stepped forward, his face inches away from her beautiful flesh.

He hardened at the scent of her, at the sight of her, and he was disgusted at himself. He was aroused at the sight of his naked woman, the one he'd brutalized with his selfish pursuit of pleasure.

But yes, he was sure that the color had changed from pure black to matted purple.

He straightened, running his hands through his hair, tearing out locks in frustration. He barely noticed the pain, and what he did notice, he reveled in. He deserved it, needed it—more pain. He deserved to be flayed for what he'd done. Drawn and quartered.

Especially because, even amongst his carnal pain at seeing her —*his*—bruised and broken as she was, he felt joy. It was so foreign it almost felt like an illness taking hold of his body. But it was there. Happiness. Because he had found her.

And ruined her.

He let out a growl and his claw hand ripped at the ruined curtain, tearing it down so it landed with a clatter at his feet.

"Hey! Don't ruin the décor. I had a tornado chic thing going," a throaty voice snapped from the vicinity of the bed.

He was beside her in a moment, his eyes raking over the slowly fading bruises, sensing her accelerated healing doing its work on injuries that might have even been fatal on a mortal.

He didn't know enough about witches to know how long it look for them to heal, what they could withstand. At the soonest possible moment, he'd make sure to learn. Everything that could be learned.

Her violet eyes were narrowed on him, streaked with pure silver, a signifier of the power running though her. Running through him.

His cock pulsated at the memory of that power touching him, curling around him and transferring her pleasure to his own body. At first his cells had tensed, as if they were going to be attacked by the utterly alien magic trying to enter him. But then everything in him relaxed, realizing there was nothing unnatural about it. It was right. She was right.

He struggled to fight the urge to pin her down and take her again, demand that she use her powers while his cock was inside her so he could feel her pleasure and his own.

But he steeled himself as soon as his eyes moved from the apex of her thighs to the bruises covering them.

※

SHE'D BEEN awake for a handful of moments before she'd spoken. At first, she hadn't said anything because she was confused as all fuck, and her broken body smarted more than a little. She'd fixed the worst of it with a healing spell. She could've taken away all of it if she so wished, because despite feeling utterly spent and ruined, she was also *juiced.*

Pulsating with so much power she barely even recognized it. Not because she didn't have the power already, but because the source of this wasn't wrong and cold and malevolent like whatever it was lurking in the depths of her grave-stained soul.

No, this was vibrant, pulsating with life and heat.

It had come from them.

From *him.*

From the him who was butt naked and treating her to a view of the most glorious and sculpted ass she had ever seen. Seriously, she could've served cheese on that thing. And the thighs. Wow. David had nothing on this guy. Every inch was strong, corded muscle. He did not skip leg day.

As her eyes had moved up, her appreciation had turned to something else when she'd seen the warped and knotted scars covering the entirety of his muscled back.

And there was a lot of real estate there. The wolf was huge. Werewolves were notoriously built, hence a lot of them earning millions for sports teams around the world—cheating in her opinion, but she cheated life regularly, so she wasn't one to talk. But this one was something else. Large. Unyielding. Almost invincible-looking.

But *something* had been taken to him.

A whip. Of many things.

And it needed to have either almost killed him or repeatedly torn into flesh that rapidly healed for it to scar his immortal skin.

Cold rage simmered at the base of her spine at the thought of someone hurting her wolf. She ached for their blood, to burn their homes and families—wait, did she just think *her wolf?*

The clattering of the curtain chased away such dangerous thoughts.

"Hey! Don't ruin the décor. I had a tornado chic thing going," she said, forcing her voice to be light, any thoughts of before absent from the tone.

In one long blink he was no longer facing away from her at the window. He was there, right up in her space like in the alley.

But unlike in the alley, he was naked.

And *fuck*, was he naked.

She knew he was hung because of the delightful ache between her thighs, but she was glad she hadn't had too much time to inspect how hung before, because it would've scared her.

And she didn't scare easily.

Especially at penis.

But this one would've had her clenching with unease slightly, with a fear he wouldn't fit.

But he did fit.

Perfectly.

The mere memory of it had her stomach quickening with need.

He seemed to be on the same wavelength, as his cock twitched.

Then something in his aura changed from thick desire to … shame? Regret? Pain.

His wild eyes traveled all over her body. In appreciation, of course—he was only inhuman—but something else.

She followed his eyes and realized most of her body was covered in bruises in various stages of healing. She was surprised at just how many there were. Sure, she'd been in pain, but nothing crazy. A training day with Scott hurt more.

Scott.

Something inside her softened at the pure depth of his concern, not communicated by words—he didn't seem to be much of a talker—but by his entire being. The way he held his body, the energy that pulsated around him.

"Dude, no worries. This is nothing," she said, trying to reassure him and not knowing why. "I've had worse training with my halfling friend." She paused. "Shit, I hope I haven't called him a friend to his face. That would give him a complex. Then he'd think he could do stuff like braid my hair and watch Reese Witherspoon movies. Don't get me wrong, I love Reese, but that's kind of like a secret pleasure, you know? Fucks with my street cred if my enemies know I like chick flicks." She narrowed her eyes. "That means you forget that I said that," she demanded.

He didn't say a word, merely stared at her in that intense soulful way that was freaking her out once more now that the post-coitus glow was receding.

Fuck.

What had she done?

Her eyes went around her apartment, at the absolute carnage she'd wrought. It looked like an earthquake had hit, then a hurricane, and then some looters had breezed through.

"Fuck," she whispered, pushing up. She hissed as the pain she thought she wasn't feeling made an appearance.

The wolf immediately moved her into his arms as if she were china.

She struggled on forced reflex, not on instinct. She hated that some part of her liked that tenderness, craved more of it, which was precisely why she fought so hard against it.

His arms turned into vises, immediately stopping her limbs from striking out at him. He was using his strength against her, of course. That's what these males did. She grinned as she got the opportunity to show him that strength wasn't all about big muscles and the ability to turn into an overgrown dog.

Blue erupted from her palms and sank into his skin, slithering underneath it. He immediately tensed, throat letting out a low rumble at the pain.

What he didn't do was let her go.

Sophie narrowed her eyes. She'd hit him with enough juice to take down a small elephant.

But she was still caught up in his arms—in his *naked* arms.

So she upped to it *two* large elephants.

Then he let her go.

She landed gracefully on her feet as he twitched against the pain. A part of her twitched as well, burning her cells for causing him pain.

She pushed that away.

He recovered quickly, standing immediately. She held up her glowing palms just in case he got any more ideas.

His jaw became granite as he stood stock-still. It took everything she had not to perve at him.

"Heal yourself," he demanded after a long and erotic silence.

Her palms still crackled, more for her sake than his. She was worried she might launch herself at him and ride him like that mechanical bull at her favorite bar.

She tilted her head, surprised he had finally spoken. She was sure she'd have to proverbially blink first.

Again, his voice was rough, wild, as if it wasn't used often. There was a slight accent she couldn't place, though wherever he was from, it sounded sexy as hell.

And the fact that he was a six-foot Adonis standing naked in front of her helped too.

"What?" she asked, so distracted by his nakedness and voice that she didn't rightly understand.

His jaw ticked again in what looked like irritation. Red spiked through his energy, a different kind of anger that had been directed inward before. This was going outward to her.

That pissed her off slightly. He was the one who had gone all Christian Grey in her shit—not that she minded, of course. A couple of broken bones were a small price to pay for some life-changing orgasms, but she should still technically be angry at him.

"You have command over considerable witchcraft," he snapped. His eyes went around the room quickly to make his point, then to her palms, then back to her eyes. They'd taken a small detour at her breasts, and her nipples had hardened immediately. "Use this power to heal yourself."

She pursed her lips and her palms glowed brighter. "I might've heard wrong, you know, through the headache caused by a cracked skull courtesy of *you,* but it sounds like you were trying to boss me around," she said evenly.

He crossed his arms and his muscles flexing as he did so.

Sophie applauded herself for keeping her scowl. And also for not drooling.

"Of course I was commanding you," he snapped. "You're my woman. You listen to me. Heal yourself."

The blue shot forward on instinct. She felt no guilt at his hiss of pain. "Whoa. See, there was a lot wrong with what you just said," she clipped, her voice changing as anger and magic swirled within it. "But here's one thing you'll learn about me that everyone else has had to learn the extreme hard way." She shot out another bolt. "The hard way makes *that* look like a hand job, just in case I'm not being clear enough," she said, smiling at his grimace of pain. "The lesson is 'don't try and boss Sophie around if you're attached to your favorite appendages.'" She looked down. "And even for a wolf, that's impressive, so I'm guessing you're attached to your pride and joy." Her eyes snapped up. "You fucked me. You broke a couple of bones, but I'm not holding that against you because I was a participating party in that horizontal tango and I wasn't complaining."

Her palms continued to grow with power, with the need to hurt, to destroy. She tamped it down.

"But penetration does not mean ownership, capisce?" She ignored whatever part of her called bullshit as she remembered how violently she'd thought of him as hers. "You wolves are an intense lot, hence the fact that I've not bedded one in my time on this hunk of rock. And this is why I won't be doing it again." She stepped forward, letting her magic whip around her in threat. "And this isn't me playing hard to get, or the start of some adorable back and forth where you chase the girl and she finally surrenders and you live happily ever after. I don't do happily ever afters. They give me a stomachache. And I *don't* surrender." She shot out another burst of power. "I *do* kill people who don't listen to me. So you should probably do that—listen, that is—and then you should probably leave."

His eyes turned to a dark amber, still glowing but with something different, something that changed with every word Sophie uttered. There was pain in them, a considerable amount since Sophie hadn't been gentle—but hey, he hadn't either—but not an ounce of fear as she'd expected. Even the most hardened immortals blanched when she let the power, her true power, seep out from its cage.

Isla hid it well, but Sophie knew it freaked even her out. And the vamp didn't freak easily, or at all.

He stood, and Sophie stepped back in shock. He shouldn't have been able to do that. His legs should've been nothing more than Jell-O until Sophie wished it different.

But there he was, standing, proving her wrong.

He didn't advance on her like she expected—and secretly hoped he would do. No, he merely stood there, staring.

She gritted her teeth. She would not talk first this time.

The silent challenge played on, both of them naked. It would've been quite comical if Sophie had been removed from the situation.

She loved laughing at Isla and the tangles she'd gotten into with males of late. She'd always wondered why Isla had threatened to dismember her and feed her to sharks when she'd teased her.

Now she got it.

"You are a strong one," he said finally, voice scratchy and low. "A fighter. Maybe even equal to me in a fight." His aura wrapped around her. "But that does not mean I will not fight. Because now that we have coupled, there is no going back, mate. This is for eternity. Until death."

She swallowed ash at the certainty in his tone, the cold passion. He believed he was right.

Fuck, I'm his mate.

"Well, death might have to be the option behind door number two, because I'm definitely not knocking at the first one," she hissed, flaring her palms in warning.

He bared his teeth, not in threat but in some kind of gruesome grin. "Ah, not even my fighter witch will kill me. I know this."

She hated the certainty in his tone. Despised that he was right. Though not entirely. Yes, *this* Sophie wouldn't kill him. The Sophie who loved Metallica concerts, combat boots, red lipstick, bad Chinese food, killing demons for sport, dismembering vampires and taunting slayers. One who also hated mushrooms and anything that was on the *E!* channel. *That* Sophie would not kill him.

But the other Sophie, the one borne from the grave, with ancient powers that had come from death itself—there was no such certainty where she was concerned. Considering she would have to kill the aforementioned original and awesome version of Sophie to gain control, the wolf had no chance against her.

He stepped forward, braving the power she shot at him for the advance. "You are mine. This does not change. And I will not leave you alone. Not until the earth crashes into the sun."

And on that vow, he was gone, snatching at what remained of his clothes as he left.

Chapter Three

"Witch, are you okay?" Isla demanded, draining her drink in one swallow, then draining Sophie's untouched one. "Please tell me you didn't go into the future and see me with *bangs*," her vampire bestie demanded with horror.

Sophie gave her a look. "Yes, because if I had ventured to the future lately—which I haven't, by the way—the most horrifying thing would be you getting an unfortunate haircut," she said dryly.

"Um, duh, have you seen my bone structure?" Isla hissed. "Flawless, but not made for bangs. It would be the biggest tragedy to unfold like *ever*."

Sophie grinned and tapped the bar so two more drinks appeared. She made sure to snatch hers before the vamp could get any ideas. "Yes, and the war we're on the brink of wouldn't even factor in."

Isla waved her hand in dismissal.

After she'd finished her drink—in two seconds—she put her whole focus on Sophie. Which was a bad thing. Isla was a huge narcissist, with little to no empathy or compassion. Which was why Sophie and her got on so well. But—and she would behead you for trying to tell anyone this—she was loyal to a fault and would fight to the death for those she considered friends.

And she also saw a lot when she took it upon herself to look. She didn't look often because she was selfish, and because she was all about fun. Seeing her friends upset was "a huge bummer, and I don't need bummers."

"Something is going on," she deduced.

Sophie sighed. "Really? The rebel faction of immortals turning humans into gross hybrids and taking over the world? Or Hell freezing over and you falling in love, with a human *slayer*, of all people, and then somehow catching the eye of the king of your entire race, which may or may not mean a death match between two really hot guys."

The death match had been on hold for the last two months since the king was in Europe, giving them a break from his hotness and annoying certainty that he thought he could tell them what to do just because he was the king of all vampires.

That meant Sophie had to tell Isla about the death spell.

Which she'd do… tomorrow.

Isla scowled and her fangs elongated in warning. "Careful, witch. Sarcasm is deadly."

Sophie tilted her head. "How is it you're still alive, then?"

She grinned, showing fang, despite the humans around them. Sophie had already cast a glamor over them to make them all but invisible. A lot less supernatural and a lot less hot.

They'd get nothing done otherwise.

"Well, an entire rebel faction is trying their darndest," she said sweetly. Her phone buzzed and she glanced down at it, rolling her eyes as she read it. Her fingers were a blur as she wrote a reply. "Thorne," Isla said by explanation, throwing the phone down and locking her emerald eyes with Sophie's. "Seriously, he can't even be away from me for like five seconds since, you know…."

"It became apparent that every supernatural being involved in a plot to overthrow a monarchy and enslave humanity wanted you dead?" Sophie asked dryly.

Isla nodded. "Yeah. Like dude, I'm still undead. Get over it already, it'll all work out."

Sophie quirked her brow. She had noticed how quickly Isla had replied at the slight change in her energy with the simple text.

A small bout of jealousy sparked through her soul. She flinched inwardly. Since when was she jealous of a happy—or in Isla's case, not entirely happy but entirely designed by fate—couple?

Since never.

Since a certain wolf had fucked the sense out of her and then declared her his, apparently.

"Well, you have almost died more than usual," Sophie said, getting herself another drink in an effort to push away unwelcome thoughts. Like large hands that morphed into claws, golden eyes, scarred physique. That kind of thing.

Isla eyed her draining her drink with a knowing gaze. "Enough talk about my death. I'm simply *bored* of it," she declared. "There's something going down. I can smell it."

Sophie wondered if she had 'I fucked a werewolf and liked it' tattooed on her forehead for the world to see, or if, for once, Isla was being perceptive about something other than Alexander McQueen's aesthetic for fall.

Sophie quirked her brow again. "The only thing you can smell is bullshit, since you're so familiar with it," she shot. "Stop trying to distract yourself from your responsibilities by making up problems in my life."

Isla scowled. "Making up problems?" she repeated. "I'm pretty sure the giant ball of crazy hocus pocus brewing in your hot little bod can be considered a problem. Especially when you start talking like that hot elf with the cool dress in *Lord of the Rings* when she got all creepy and power hungry." She narrowed her eyes. "And if you tell Scott I made a *Lord of the Rings* reference, I will skin you alive." She glanced down at her phone again as it buzzed. "And there's also the small matter of you bopping back and forth in the space-time continuum and not even coming back with any interesting souvenirs or at the very least fucking up the future as we know it," she pouted. "And I'm guessing there's a coven of witch bitches sensing the shift in the force or whatever it is you have. They've already got more than a few bones to pick with you—"

"Most of which are because of skeletons you created," Sophie interrupted.

Isla shrugged and pointed her bloodred finger at her exposed cleavage. "Vampire, remember? Murder is part and parcel. Plus, you almost always helped me."

Sophie rolled her eyes, hoping Isla was going to finish it there and get distracted by her own life, or at the very least her own reflection.

No such luck.

"They've been gunning for you for decades, Soph," she continued. "You know it because you're a badass bitch. Some of it could be because of a couple of very small and hardly noticeable explosions and civil wars I had a small hand in." She held her thumb and finger millimeters apart. "But mostly it's because you don't toe the line, didn't at Hogwarts or wherever it is baby witches learn their shit. And then you moved out of the great coven, abandoned the caldrons for whisky bottles and then started a business working with all immortals, no matter their beef with your sisters, and making a lot of bank off it." She grinned. "All of this I approve of, greatly. And we both know anything I approve of usually spells trouble. For once, you don't even need me for trouble. They're power hungry, your bunch. Not unlike my family. We both have assholes who are related to us who want to use us for something or kill us. Just because the spotlight hasn't been on you doesn't make your threat any less important. It's just because I'm a drama queen and take the stage."

Her eyes flickered with something foreign, something serious. Concern?

"I'm worried about you, Hermione," she said softly. "Almost as much as I'm worried about myself."

Sophie laughed off whatever uncomfortable form of premonition Isla's words had brought forward. "You never worry about someone as much as you worry about yourself."

Isla flicked her hair, the serious expression giving way to the sardonic smile that was so much more welcome to Sophie. "I know, that's why I said *almost*." She tapped at her phone. "You want to expand as to where these powers actually came from? I think we skipped right over that part when we went to prophecies that didn't make any fucking sense." Isla screwed up her nose.

Sophie knew she hated the prophecy that put her smack-dab in the middle of what was gearing up to be the greatest war of their times.

Isla loved to be the center of attention, but hated being told what to do. Especially by gods.

And there was a little inkling Sophie had that she was somehow smack-dab in the middle of all this too. Her powers gave her the ability to sense when her life was going to be threatened, and there was an aching certainty that her entire existence hung in the balance.

Cemented when the wolf came into all this.

Isla looked to the door, her scowl deepening. "Seriously," she muttered. "I feel like I need to get a restraining order."

Sophie glanced over to the hulking man making his way over to them. Every single female eye—and half of the males—were on him as he reached them, and then when he entered Sophie's glamor, the humans blinked in confusion for a few seconds before resuming their boring lives.

Thorne's eyes hadn't moved from Isla the entire time, as if he might topple off the side of the earth if he didn't keep his gaze on the vampire.

And then his lips brushed the side of her neck in a decidedly intimate way that made even Sophie squirm. There was something about the two of them that radiated an energy that was hard to weather. Something so ancient, something so strong.

Sophie was happy for her friend, despite all the blood and gore that was coming with the courtship—it was Isla, after all—but she hated that all this had made her inspect the decidedly empty and blackened heart she'd carried around for the past few decades.

Not quite empty, something inside her whispered, taunting her with golden eyes.

"Sophie," Thorne greeted in his gravelly voice.

She grinned away her unease. "Hey, Buffy."

His jaw instantly hardened and Isla's smile widened. She lived —kind of—to piss Thorne off. Though her act didn't fool Sophie. The vampire had it bad.

"You were not supposed to crash girls' night," Isla snapped. "It's like an ancient law."

Thorne eyed his woman. "Don't give a fuck about ancient traditions, baby," he murmured. Sex lingered in his voice, an invitation for Isla only. Eyes for Isla only.

Isla was the only thing that kept the human's heart beating.

Sophie had the ability to see concrete and unbreakable ties between people, and this was the strongest she'd ever encountered. If this was severed, not only would each of their immortal lives end, but the world quite possibly would too.

Talk about pressure.

Isla immediately jumped off her stool, snatching her Chanel. "I know I always say chicks before dicks, but you haven't seen his dick. It really is something special." She gave her a wink. "Catch you on the flipside, motherfucker."

Then either Thorne or Isla dragged the other out.

Sophie watched them leave, unease swirling inside her.

Then she put her attention back to the two fresh drinks in front of her. The best way to get over the end of the world was to get drunk.

After five more drinks, the end of the world thing didn't seem as important as before. But she couldn't get the wolf dilemma from her head. Or her vagina, which *missed* him.

The werewolf *mated* her. And not just in the biblical sense of the word. Werewolves and demons were the only supernatural species who had one true 'mate' that was designed to be theirs and only theirs for the rest of eternity.

Sophie always kind of got it with wolves, pack animals and all that. Demons, she didn't. That meant they were capable of love, and they came from Hades himself. It was somewhat of a contradiction. Though she had yet to meet a demon who cared about anything other than collecting souls, so maybe it was a myth.

Wolves, on the other hand, were notorious for their devotion to their mates.

For eternity.

And she had inadvertently *mated* with one.

She couldn't even commit to a nail polish color for one day, let alone a partner for... forever.

A *wolf* partner at that.

Great, so she'd thought the only bad consequences of being easy were the stage-five clingers who *all* became her stalkers on account of her being excellent in bed.

Pregnancy was never a worry since being a witch meant contraception was a simple spell that required little to no energy.

And then even when the immortals she'd bedded became obsessed with her, she'd merely erased their memories of her. Slightly harder than the contraception, considering she made an impression and wasn't easy to forget.

She'd tried it already with this wolf, but it was like trying to push a mountain into a Mini Cooper. Not gonna happen, and also just embarrassing.

No, even her ever-growing magic was no match for the werewolf mating instinct. That was something so natural, so ingrained into their being, she'd have to practice the darkest, blackest magic in order to pry herself from his soul.

It would mean damning herself to the order of the big bad witches with ties to the Devil.

She hadn't ruled it out just yet.

And she couldn't tell Isla. No way, no how. Her vampire bestie wasn't about to judge her for getting biblical with a guy she didn't know the name of considering she'd done it on the daily with men throughout the centuries—well, before she got all gross and loved-up with her slayer, that was.

No, Isla would likely judge her on the fact that the one-night stand was a werewolf. One who had recognized her as his mate, and by boinking him, she'd cemented their connection without knowing it until it was too late.

Great. Because I couldn't keep it in my pants, I'm bound to a werewolf for eternity unless one of us dies.

§

SOPHIE HAD no idea what time it was when she stumbled into her elevator. She knew how many drinks it had been, though.

No, that was a lie. She had no idea how many drinks it had been, but she did know it was the perfect amount. Nothing seemed like a big deal anymore. Potential end of the world and largest war the immortal community had ever experienced? Great way to get rid of frenemies plaguing her life.

Witch coven gunning for her submission and perhaps even her

imprisonment? Easy peasy, set the whole place on fire and watch them burn.

Werewolf seemingly set on the fact that she was his lifelong mate? Hire a good dog catcher. Or put rat poison in his kibble.

Everything was simple, apart from using the elevator. It took her three tries to make contact with the buttons, and then she pressed all the wrong ones. But she got to her floor eventually. She needed a code to get in, since her loft opened straight off the elevator.

That was tricky.

In the end, she used a spell to open it.

"Open sesame!" she shouted at the closed doors.

That one only works in mortal movies, idiot, the soberest part of her—which was still pretty wasted—told her.

"Drat, right," she whispered.

It took some doing, but she got the right spell and the elevator doors finally opened. Good thing too, because she needed to pee.

"Sesame is open!" she shouted at her empty apartment.

A spike in her power and an immediate rising of her proverbial hackles told her that her apartment was not empty.

She stared at the intruder standing right in front of her.

"I've really got to change my spells to make sure they kill anyone who tries to get in here," she hissed. "Or at the very least makes all their hair fall out."

Hazel pursed her lips in disapproval. As if her face had any other expression.

"You know, you're meant to suck on lemons *after* having a tequila shot," Sophie slurred. "Not just, you know, all day errday."

Hazel's brown eyes were saturated with disdain.

Sophie's were too. At her outfit. Was she seriously wearing tweed?

"You're drunk," Hazel spat at her.

"Am I?" Sophie exclaimed in shock. "Oh my gosh, alcohol

makes you *drunk*? I thought it was to make idiotic people bearable. It's only working on one of those counts." She grinned. "Guess which." She leaned forward. "I'll give you a clue. You're still unbearable," she stage-whispered.

Hazel sighed. "I don't have time for this."

"Well isn't that great," Sophie said, stepping away from the path to the elevator. "The door is right there."

"I'm not leaving without you," Hazel said, her power flickering in threat.

Sophie yearned to answer.

"The coven sent me to bring you back. We can't let this stand anymore," Hazel continued. "Your partnership with *vampires*. Your mercenary ways. Refusing to use your power for the good of the coven." She gazed at her outfit. Sophie had on a Guns N' Roses tee she'd cut to have the perfect amount of underboob, high-waisted leather jeans and platform Doc Martins.

"Your lack of taste, of *discretion*," Hazel spat.

She stepped forward, as if she was trying to be menacing. Sophie smirked. No one could be menacing in tweed. Even with the considerable amount of power that seeped from her former teacher's eyes. "We can sense your power growing. We will not stand for your gift to be squandered, to be used in help of the enemy. The power belongs to all witches. For the greater good. I have been instructed to use any means necessary to bring you back to where you belong."

Sophie laughed off the shot of magic that Hazel had directed at her. "Really?" she said in response. "I'm off-my-face drunk and that was easier than pressing an elevator button." Sophie stepped forward, letting her own power eat away at Hazel's, snap at the shards of it. She found great satisfaction in the fact that the other witch stepped back, fear coloring her aura.

She's afraid of me. She's afraid because she can sense what's inside me and it terrifies her.

That makes two of us.

"You really think it's gonna be as easy as shooting a binding spell at me when I'm piss drunk, or asking rudely for me to come back to a place I hate, full of witches I despise?" she asked, stumbling slightly.

Fuck, that totally messes with the whole menacing vibe I've got going. She set her curtains on fire to compensate.

Hazel's eyes flickered upward and then to Sophie. "You cannot control this, Sophie."

Sophie laughed. "Maybe not. But neither can you, despite what you think. I know which choice is going to be more fun, and it's going to be the one where I make you run back to the coven without your eyebrows... and with a snout," Sophie decided.

She had been just about to cast that very spell when her instincts sensed something in the elevator.

Someone.

Her heart beat a little faster, and her palms dampened.

It was her wolf.

And then a cinderblock hit her square in the chest and she went flying right into the opening doors of the elevator, crashing into the wolf's arms painfully.

She tasted his fury immediately and he put her down on shaky feet, shoving her behind him with glowing eyes.

Sophie recovered quickly, using her magic to push him aside. "Really?" she asked the half-turned wolf. "You think you're going to be saving me on the reg just because we've fucked?" She shook her head and sent a burst of power forth, smashing Hazel into her dining room table, not moving her gaze from golden eyes. "Yeah, not gonna happen. I'm an independent witch, and a powerful one at that. Not only am I capable of fighting my own battles, I enjoy doing so."

On that, she stepped out of the elevator just in time for the doors to shut in front of the wolf. She bound them closed, and the metal groaned against his body slamming itself against it.

Slightly more sober, Sophie ignored her broken chest bone and sauntered to the mess in front of her where Hazel was crumpled.

"Now I get why Isla is so pissy all the time," she said, taking stock of the shattered remains of her ten-thousand-dollar dining table. "This is just *annoying*."

Hazel was bleeding from her forehead, a bone was jutting out from her wrist and her juice was severely weakened. Sophie couldn't believe that she used to think this woman was one of the strongest witches she knew—and also the biggest twat. She'd quite literally wiped her dining room table with her, while almost blind drunk, no less.

"If you're going to come for a battle, then at least come prepared next time," Sophie said, using her power to lift Hazel to her feet. "This is just embarrassing."

Hazel's eyes went to where guttural growls sounded from the doors struggling against the wolf's effort, even with Sophie's enchantment. He was pushing past it. Which should have been impossible, but it was kind of hard to miss the fist-shaped indentation in the metal, which was only growing larger.

"You're aligned with the *wolves* now?" Hazel gasped.

Sophie shrugged. "I guess we'll find out when he breaks through. He'll either rip you to pieces. Or me." She clapped. "The anticipation is *killing* me."

Hazel's true fear permeated the room. She took one more glance at the doors that were about to give way, then back to Sophie. "This isn't over."

Sophie rolled her eyes. "Way to sound like every pathetic villain in every B-grade movie, dude."

There was a large concentration of magic as Hazel pressed a crystal she was wearing on her wrist, then sank into the air.

Ah, so she had a magical escape route. Such a charm required a lot of power. Likely the whole coven had to contribute to it.

All for little old Sophie. That was just flattering.

It was that moment that her spell and the elevator doors gave way and the wolf sprinted into Sophie's apartment, wild eyes desperately searching for the threat, claws extended and form lengthening as he prepared to fully change.

Man and beast eyes focused on her.

"Little too late, wolf," she said. "I already saved myself. Doesn't that just piss you off?"

His anger and need saturated every part of her skin, his eyes focusing on her chest, as if he could sense the broken bones there. Which of course was stupid. On this rare occasion, she'd covered up her cleavage, so there was no way for him to see the no doubt angry bruises she'd be sporting.

Good thing she was drunk; otherwise, they'd hurt a lot more. Also, bad thing she was drunk, because she wasn't likely up to a spell to heal herself.

"If you'll excuse me, I'm going to go throw up now," she informed him, sauntering toward her bathroom with a sway to her hips to counteract the statement.

He was still there after she'd emptied her stomach, splashed cold water on her face—only making herself look like Alice Cooper, since heavy kohl was her signature—and brushed her teeth.

She groaned as she made a beeline for her fridge.

He was in front of her, barring her access to cold beer and the leftover Chinese that she was sure would still be good.

Ah, so the wolf wanted to die today.

"You are intoxicated," he said, voice a low growl as he was still in the process of ridding himself of the change.

Sophie wondered idly how difficult it was to put the beast back inside the cage. It looked pretty fucking hard. Plus his aura was tight, almost concrete with exertion. As were his muscles.

They're hot muscles, she noted.

She folded her arms, flinching at the motion, and his entire body responded. "Why does everyone keep pointing out that I'm drunk like I don't know?" Sophie asked. "*I* was the one spelling the bartender to give me my drinks. I'm aware I'm trashed. It was kind of the point."

She leaned forward, not to get a whiff of his utterly male scent but to make the narrowing of her eyes that much more menacing.

"And it was all your fault, actually." She flinched again, gesturing to her ruined apartment. "This was *all* your fault, in fact," she hissed. "Before you came along with your intense stare and your glorious dick, my apartment was kickass, and I only had an apocalypse and some ancient witches and hybrid factions plus a rebel army to deal with. That was *cake* compared to this." She waved her hand between them, flinching again as the motion rebroke a rib that had just knitted back together.

His body was steel, now completely male and completely beautiful. He was only wearing a black tee, ripped at the torso, where she could see a peek of an ab. She ached to see its brothers, but this was not the time. His knuckles were torn and bloodied, though rapidly healing.

His jeans were still perfect, a slight coppery stain, but other than that, nothing. How could he go through bashing his way through an elevator door and not get a mark on them when Sophie couldn't even eat a hot dog without getting a mustard stain on *something.*

Oh, a hot dog would be killer right now.

"You're injured," he said through gritted teeth, pure fury radiating from his very pores.

It was super hot.

"Another thing I'm aware of," Sophie snapped, wondering if she was sober enough to render him unconscious, transport him to the Baltic Sea and conjure herself a hot dog from the stand down the street.

No, she only had the sobriety and the power for one of those things.

"Well, heal yourself," he demanded.

Sophie took a bite out of her hot dog, the ketchup spurting onto the toe of her shoe. "No, I can't do that, on account of the whole drunk thing you pointed out before," she said between bites.

His eyes had widened slightly when the hot dog had appeared out of thin air, though it seemed he had bigger issues with Sophie than her conjuring a hot dog for her and not for him.

She licked her fingers as she polished it off. "Oh, I'm sorry, were you hungry?" she asked, mindful of his eyes on her fingers and her mouth, the mood of the room changing rapidly. "I would've got you one too, just didn't know how you felt about the whole 'dog' portion of the equation."

She was in his arms before she even knew what hit her.

"I'm hungry, *mo spéir*," he growled, striding through Sophie's apartment and somehow gliding, as if on air, so her chest didn't jolt. "But not for anything humans can create or give me." His eyes burned into her, freezing both her and her magic in place. "Only one can sate me."

The stark light of Sophie's bathroom jolted her out of whatever spell he had cast with his words. *She* was meant to be the *fricking* witch, damnit.

"No, I'm not doing any sating, now or ever," she hissed, struggling in his arms despite the pain.

His iron grip paralyzed her. "You do not move, lest you aggravate your injuries more," he clipped, somehow keeping hold of her and leaning over to turn the taps of her vintage claw-footed tub. "I do not know how long it takes witchlings to heal, but from what I have witnessed, you are stronger than any of your kind," he continued, in the longest speech she'd heard from the wolf since she'd met him. And then fucked him. And then almost killed him with her magic.

Now there he was, running Sophie a *bath*.

"I am no healer, and since you admit you're too intoxicated to do so, you will bathe and I will ensure I do everything in my power to sober you up enough so your injuries no longer contort your fucking face in agony." He lost whatever cool his tone had betrayed, the air seeming to simmer with his fury.

"It's not agony," Sophie argued. "Just mildly uncomfortable suffering."

This did not help. "You are *mine*. You do not suffer."

She froze at the words, at that concrete thread she'd seen just that night in someone else, attaching itself to her.

Nuh-uh, not happening.

"I am *not* yours," she gritted out as steam filled the bathroom.

He ignored her, tracing his thumbs along the highs of her cheeks, then downward, trailing the side of her neck, the pads of his fingers rough and gentle at the same time.

The touch made her shiver despite the growing warmth in the room, despite the inferno that seemed to reside under his skin.

Her tee slid off her shoulders, revealing the beginning of the sleeve she'd had inked there as soon as tattoos had become refined and hygienic. Magic helped with the way the illustrations were almost living paintings on her arms.

The wolf's eyes glowed even brighter as his large finger trailed the decaying castle that housed a skeletal princess, butterflies crowning her corpse.

She ached for him to explore every piece of ink on her skin—with his tongue, preferably—but the movement of her tee had also revealed a stark purple that she had not gotten from a tattooist needle.

He hissed out a vicious breath, immediately setting her on her feet so his claws could cleave through the scant fabric of her tee and reveal the extent of her injury.

Hazel's spell had been sheer energy, kind of like throwing a bowling ball at someone's clavicle. Even though Sophie's healing was accelerated and her pain threshold was high, and she was still as drunk as a skunk, it fucking hurt.

Sophie knew it would only get worse as the bones knitted themselves together; breaking something wasn't nearly as painful as healing what was broken.

She couldn't heal herself with a spell with alcohol running through her blood—a witch must have clean blood in order to cast spells on herself—but there was a sobering potion she was a dab hand at since she routinely drank and then just as routinely did magic on herself.

Nothing for vanity's sake, but she hung around with Isla, was a mercenary for mortals and immortals alike, and she fucked her body up on the reg, so magical healing was necessary. Otherwise broken bones took *days* to heal.

But she couldn't make her potion now, because she had an angry werewolf in front of her and she'd used her last stock of eye of newt.

Though she'd never admit to Isla that she actually used that ingredient.

"I will end the witch," the wolf declared, his fury palpable as his eyes were attached to her chest.

Sophie frowned because he'd taken off her shirt and she wasn't wearing a bra. She wasn't uncomfortable, or modest—she had a great rack. No, she was perturbed by the fact that the male was glued to her injury instead of her great tits.

"Well that would be nice," she said. "But other matters are more pressing at this juncture." She narrowed her eyes at him as steam made the room murky, ominous. Beads of perspiration formed between her breasts. He noticed *that*, his desire soaking through fury in a beautiful marriage that had Sophie wet, despite it all.

"I am *not* your mate," she said firmly.

His eyes dragged themselves from her nipples, which had hardened. She expected an argument. That's what these alphas did, wasn't it? Yelled 'You are mine' until the poor woman got so annoyed she relented because it was easier, and more often than not, the immortal was hot. And great in the sack.

The wolf was both of those things.

But Sophie would not relent.

She could not relent.

Instead of shouting, beating his chest, or pissing in a circle around her, he stepped to the bath, turning the taps off. He pushed her back against the small lip of her large tub, giving her enough room to slide the edge of her butt onto it while he lifted her legs and yanked at her boots.

They didn't budge, obviously, because of intricate laces she'd secured with multiple knots. She'd dressed for a quiet drink with Isla, which meant she'd needed to make sure her footwear was secure enough that it wouldn't fly off when she round-housed a demon. Or a hybrid, or, goddess willing, Isla's family.

Any of those things she'd envisaged that night. She had not imagined a werewolf to be literally kneeling at her feet and undressing her.

His claws cut through the laces instead of taking the time to untie them—typical brute—and he yanked off both the boots and her socks.

Instead of immediately moving upward, he retracted his claws and kneaded his callused hands into the soles of her feet.

Sophie threw her head back and let out a little moan. Normally she would not be about a guy giving her a foot massage—she hated people touching her feet, gross!—but whether it be the booze or the man in front of her, it was sheer ecstasy.

She had never expected a werewolf, and this wild one in particular, to be able to take such care of a woman by doing something as beta as a foot massage, but the wolf took his time, worked relentlessly as if it was the most important job in the world.

Sophie was not complaining.

She was on her feet once more, the soft bath mat curling around her toes. The wolf's hands trailed up the leather of her pants, circling her thighs to press the pads of his fingers into her ass.

He let out a low growl in his throat, she guessed in appreciation for her well-formed buttocks, or maybe the way the leather of these pants hugged it like a second skin. Whatever it was sent need shooting between Sophie's legs.

Every part of him—including his most important part—hardened as Sophie's panties dampened, as if he could sense it.

The laces at the front of her pants suffered the same fate as those of her boots. She didn't even find it in her to complain. Especially since he peeled them over her hipbones, kneeling as he did so, his face almost buried in the lace of her panties.

Another guttural growl. His desire seeped into her skin, fueling her own, weakening her knees and building a climax that didn't even need his touch to stoke.

His breath was hot through the thin lace of her panties, and she let out a low moan as the air teased her sensitive flesh, crying out for his touch. He didn't give it to her, the thing every one of her cells was aching for. She knew he was aching for it too, every emotion flowing through him stark, etched in his features, in the energy surrounding him.

His lips pressed into her panties and he sucked in a breath through his nose, *smelling* her. She should have been embarrassed at such an intimate gesture but it only made her crazier with need, especially when the growl of appreciation in his throat warmed her to her very bones.

Then he moved lower, her pants moving down her legs with agonizing slowness. He took his time, tracing the skin of her thighs with his eyes, staring at the tattoos that snaked upward and downward, the snake that curled up the side of her thigh, its scales intricate ancient runes, flowers tangling around its body.

The journey to her ankles was the most frustrating and erotic-filled moments Sophie had ever experienced. The experience itself was in direct conflict with everything she'd thought the wolf to be. The need barely restrained in his body—plus her previous knowledge of wolves—told her that he should've been wildly taking her, brutally, with absolute ferocity, with no control, much like he had before.

Her panties dampened at the mere thought of it. The flex of his hands against her ankles told her he noticed.

But he did not move. She could almost feel the beast tearing at her; she couldn't even imagine the battle for him. Never in her life did she think she'd actually *want* a werewolf to lose control, but now she wanted nothing more than that. But her limbs were lead, her power sinking at the bottom of her stomach, and she was unable to lift it to make something happen, to wrench control into her hands.

Again the wolf had bewitched her when it was meant to be the other way around. She should've cared. By gods, she should've cared.

But then he stood and took his shirt off. And she found she didn't care.

Whatsoever.

🐾

His female was paralyzed in front of him. Trembling with a need so intense it brought him to his knees, because she deserved to be worshipped, and because he didn't trust himself if he moved toward her magnificent breasts or perfect cunt.

The beast inside him roared at such a thought. It scraped at the sides of his mind, drawing blood, tearing at his skull with the insane need to claim her. Sink his cock inside her, spill his seed, claim her forever, imprint his scent into her so deeply so she wore it like the ink that covered her body.

So no other wolf would dare touch her.

Unless they wanted to die.

But he did not do so.

Memories of her bruised and broken body lying before him after surrendering to his beast last time haunted him. He knew they would haunt him for every day that he walked this earth. And he planned on walking all those days with her.

So he had time to take her brutally as both man and the beast ached to.

But she was hurt.

Again.

The bones inside her chest—the ones protecting her fucking *heart*—had been shattered by that cumbersome witch. The one who would be getting the skin ripped from her bones. Slowly. He cared not that she was a woman. Nothing mattered when she'd harmed his mate. That was the ultimate sin, and he would have no mercy.

But first he'd take care of his witch. Of her body. Then he'd take care of that feral need that near matched his own.

Yes, this little kitten was perfect for him, even if he hadn't understood it at first. He'd always thought his mate would be another wolf, bring him back into the world he'd shunned for all these centuries, the world he'd despised. She'd give him someone to run with. Someone to shift with. Have children with.

Never would he have imagined a foulmouthed, short-haired, tattooed, and feisty witch.

But she was fucking perfect.

Her eyes ate up every inch of his torso when he ripped his shirt off. Her arousal sang in his nostrils as he scented her, getting even wetter at the sight of his body. Warmth spread through his bones, his cock hardening further. His female found him pleasing, did not shy away from his skin that was covered in scars. Her eyes glowed as power shot through them, mingling with the effects of the considerable amount of alcohol he still scented in her system.

It was enough to fell a wolf, yet she not only *walked* in that state—and talked in complete sentences—she had bested a witch, and she had done it without his help.

"Wolf," she hissed, her voice thick with need. Her black-tipped hands reached out for his jeans, and despite his determination not to unleash himself on her, he leaned forward so she could unzip him, free him.

The beast shook inside his bones as her small hands gripped his cock, her eyes glued to it in wonder.

"Gods," he ground out as she moved up and down, milking his throbbing cock. The pressure building at the base of his spine told him he'd explode if he didn't stop her. Fuck, he did not want to stop her, not right now. But he would not spend his seed in her hand. Not when she stood in front of him injured and inebriated.

He'd take her drunk, though. Another time, many times. He liked his little witch sans inhibitions. She seemed to forget she was meant to be fighting this. He liked fighting with his witch, but he reveled in her surrender.

The moment her touch became too much to bear, he circled her wrists with his hands, painfully taking them off him.

She hissed out a protest, and fuck, did he feel that in his cock too. But he made himself focus on the purple of her chest. He transferred both of her wrists to one of his hands, easily holding her in place as he kicked off his boots and yanked down his jeans.

In one swift movement, he immersed them both in the warm

water, splashing liquid onto the floor. He made sure she landed between his legs, though her hot little body against his aching shaft was the perfect kind of agony. He gritted his teeth through it as he laid her against his chest, reveling in having the wet and naked skin of his female against him.

His female.

"I can't believe you just did that," she spat, trying for irritated, but her voice still had that hypnotized dream quality to it. "You need to let me up and out of here," she demanded. "I cannot be *bathing* with a werewolf."

He grinned against her hair. She'd been fucking a werewolf not two nights before. And she'd have let that same werewolf fuck her against the wall if he hadn't stopped himself—and his beast—from doing so.

Instead, he said nothing, as he was used to. Speaking with her wasn't as painful as it was with everyone else. It was almost natural. He still had to yank the words out, but he wanted to, for her.

He didn't yank them that time because, despite her demand, she made no move to struggle from the bath. She could've done so. He also knew she could've commanded her considerable power to magic herself—or him—out if she so wished.

She was not a helpless female, his mate. She was not going to be somewhere she did not want to be. The sheer fact that her smooth back rubbed against his hard cock told him she was exactly where she wanted to be.

"A bath with a werewolf," she muttered to herself. "This isn't what badass witches like me do. This is what idiotic romantics who watch *The Notebook* and go to book clubs do," she ranted. "Imagine would Isla would say if she could see me now. At least there's no candles. That's where I'd draw the line." There was a pause. "Though candles are a good conductor for my power," she mused. "It's not like they wouldn't be here for a purpose...."

He felt the air move on her command, and the candles surrounding the surfaces in the large bathroom suddenly alighted.

He grinned even more, the expression foreign on his face, but he couldn't help doing so, listening to the little witch mutter to herself in such a way that enchanted him without any use of her magic.

"Don't get any ideas," she hissed, turning her head slightly so she could glare at him over her shoulder. His cock twitched again, and with the way her entire body shuddered, he knew she felt it. "This is, uh... just for power conductors. The candles," she said, voice not as sharp as before.

He didn't reply, didn't need to, because she turned back around and sank into his chest with a long sigh. He sensed that his woman had gone almost as long as he had without moments like this. Which was good, because he was planning on hunting down every male who had touched her and systematically executing him. He hoped there would not be a lot.

He glanced to the shelf beside the bath, snatching a shampoo bottle and squeezing its contents into his hands. Most of her black hair was drenched, and he used his free hand to cup water and pour it over the rest of her head.

She made a sound at the back of her throat as he lathered the shampoo onto her head, massaging it onto her scalp, extending his claws ever so slightly so he could scratch at her.

Another moan.

Another cock flex.

He gritted his teeth.

This was pure torture. He had waited centuries for his woman, to claim her, and there he was fucking *washing her hair*. But mates were more than just someone to spill seed into. Even the wild beast inside him wanted more than that. It was pure instinct that compelled him to care for his female in every way possible, protect her from harm—with his life, if need be—which was why his treatment of her on their first claiming haunted him so.

He deserved the torture of having her wet, naked body against him and his cock straining with the need to be inside it. She'd felt pain worse than that.

From him.

But had she really?

She'd transferred her pleasure to him while he plunged into her; he'd tasted the sheer nirvana both of them shared. Even after she woke up—before she'd turned on him, of course—she'd betrayed no true pain, no vulnerability.

She could handle it.

Broken bones, bruises, she treated them as if they were nothing. He sensed her life was violent—it was attached to her, chaos. Inked into her very skin, dancing behind her eyes. He sensed true and dangerous chaos further inside her, threaded into the magic she unleashed.

He loved that violence, because he too could not escape it. Would never escape it.

But that did not mean that was the only thing he could give her.

More water cascaded over her head as he washed the shampoo away. She groaned again, but was not content to lie docile.

He'd known it was only a matter of time before she came back to rights.

She turned in the tub, splashing more water over the edge. Despite its overly large size, it was a tight fit for the both of them, considering he was both an overly large man and an overly large werewolf.

Her eyes glowed in the dim candlelight, and he scented barely a whiff of the alcohol that had near replaced her blood before.

Surely she couldn't have metabolized it that quickly.

He glanced down at her chest, willing himself not to be

distracted by her perfect nipples. The angry red bruising had receded to a dull brown, and he sensed no broken bones that had been there moments before.

She had said the candles worked as some sort of, what was the word... conductor, but this was almost impossible.

"That's enough washing," she purred, her voice rough, pushing away all thoughts of impossible. "I think it's my turn now."

Water droplets trailed down her naked skin, glistening in the flickering light, and he had to clench the sides of the tub to stop himself from snatching her, most likely breaking bones that had just healed.

The marble cracked and neither of them noticed.

Her short hair hung like a curtain as she circled his shaft under the water.

He hissed out a curse.

Her eyes glowed with erotic satisfaction as she watched him, as she drank in his reaction to her stroking him, burning the base of his spine with his need for release once more.

It surprised him that his teeth did not shatter with the force of clenching his jaw. He had not exerted this much control over himself in his entire time on earth. He'd thought such a feat as restraining the beast in front of a naked and willing mate was impossible.

She was quickly teaching him about what was impossible.

"Wolf," she rasped again. Her hand paused and he nearly broke the sides of the tub. "I do not know your name." Her eyes were glowing now, as was her pale body. It should have disturbed him—werewolves were distrustful of witches by nature and despised witchcraft—but there was nothing to hate about his witch. About her power. "I guess I could keep calling you Wolf," she mused, "but I would like to have choices."

Her hand stayed circling the base of his shaft, unmoving, as if she was torturing the mere information of his name from him. It took him a few moments to answer because her beauty had yanked it straight from his mind.

She's literally making me forget my own fucking name.

"Conall," he growled finally, half of it coming out barely conceivable.

"Conall," she repeated, rolling the name over her tongue. His balls burned for release.

He could no longer hold onto his beast, not upon hearing his true name spoken from his mate's lips. Water splashed everywhere as he stood, snatching her as he did so. He hadn't even realized he'd shattered the marble of the tub, kicking at it in his desperation, until water flooded through the room, settling under his feet.

She didn't notice it because he'd claimed her mouth and she had wrapped her legs around his waist, grinding her sodden panties against his shaft. He'd left them on because he knew he wouldn't have been able to control himself had he seen her perfect, exposed core.

She nibbled at his bottom lip, drawing blood, and he barely stopped himself from squeezing her with enough force to break her ribs. The bed was still ruined from the last time he was there, and he threw her on it once more.

A warm wind picked up, coming from her. He sucked it in, following her to the bed, moving down her body so he could rip her panties off with his teeth.

She let out a cry as he did so and as his finger pushed inside her wetness.

"Conall!" she screamed.

His wolf howled inside him at her screaming his name on the edge of climax, with his finger inside of her.

"You shall not come until I'm inside you," he demanded. "Until you admit one thing."

She blinked at him through hooded lashes, wild with need. "I'll admit I was on the grassy knoll if that's what you need. Just come inside."

The wind roared around them, mirroring her need.

"That you are mine," he said, voice little more than a rasp. "Mine and only mine. No other being will possess you except me."

The wind stopped abruptly, snatching her scent from the air and seeming to take his oxygen with it.

Every inch of her body tensed, which caused her core to clench around his finger. She let out a cry at that, then scampered off the bed with a blinding speed for a witch.

"You need to leave, now," she demanded, voice hard.

He scowled at her, standing as quick as she did and advancing on her. His beast shimmered underneath his face, but she did not retreat.

He felt pride in the midst of his fury. She held her own. She always would. "I will not go anywhere except inside my fucking woman," he growled.

She jutted her chin up in defiance, even though he could all but taste her need from his words. Something bitter swirled in the air, something working to become a barrier from his body reaching hers. His skin rippled with the change as he fought against her magic.

Her gaze flickered as his beast started to tear through the invisible wall between them. "Even your sorcery cannot deny me," he growled. "I will have you. It will be done."

Her eyes were somehow immediately black. "You will have none of me," she promised.

He didn't speak, merely gritted his teeth and continued to gain traction against her power. Soon he'd be able to snatch her shoulders, claim her mouth, take her against the wall as he'd ached to do before.

"You're going to *rape* me, Conall?" she asked flatly.

The words were a slap.

He stilled.

"Because if you continue this, you might be able to work through my magic, but then you will force yourself inside me. And then I will have to kill you. Will you do that? Force your attentions on me?"

The words themselves sickened him, and the worst thing was her sincerity. She had wanted him moments before, had matched his crazed need. But something in his words had shut off that need and gave way to burning hatred. If he continued to fight, he would win. Then his beast would take over and he would take her. Claim her well and proper.

Rape.

The ugly word cut at his mind.

Never would he force himself on his mate. Causing her such pain was akin to a death sentence. He knew one such wolf in his old life. The one whose beast had taken over and had claimed his unwitting human mate.

She'd survived.

But she'd been broken.

That wolf had hurled himself off a cliff.

Even a hundred-foot drop could kill an immortal, Conall had discovered that day. But it wasn't the fall that had killed the wolf—that had merely ended his body. His essence was gone the second he'd defiled his mate.

She'd followed him to the grave shortly thereafter.

He tensed his body.

She stepped back from him. "You will leave now. And drunk or not, you're in my house next time, I will kill you. It is your demise that will follow any more of your advances to *mate* with me," she growled, her voice taking on a quality that was not natural to her. Something else speaking in her stead from inside her that terrified Conall.

Because he knew, inside of his heart, that whatever it was

sought to destroy his mate. And he could not kill it because it lived inside her. So he did not move.

"I swear to every goddess and deity who has gifted me with my power that I will do so," she vowed, the concreteness of the words settling into the air like some sort of binding contract.

The promise of death hung between them for a moment more. Then he swallowed acid at the thought of leaving her.

"Very well," he gritted out.

He tasted both victory and disappointment inside of her.

That meant she was not lost forever.

Just for now.

He didn't hesitate to dart into the ruined bathroom and snatch his sopping clothes. Nor to tear out the window and into the night, running as fast as his legs would take him. He had to, because if he let himself linger, the last thread of control he was clutching would snap, his beast would take over, and she would be lost forever.

He reached the woods outside of the city in record time, changing and sprinting through them to his cabin he'd hidden when he'd bought the land.

Conall was not going to give up on his mate—his witch— merely because she threatened to curse him and blow him off the face of the earth. It would take that very thing to get rid of him.

He merely had to change his strategy. Hadn't he been his clan's chief strategizer, a title he'd warmed to better than the one burned into him at birth. Though it had been centuries since he'd led his pack into wars—centuries since he had a pack—such instincts would not go away. And this was a war, with his witch. With whatever power, whatever being lay inside her that was threatening their union.

So he would not force himself into her, not taste her lips, not feel his skin against hers, though the very thought of it pained him.

He would take it upon himself to fight this battle she had been muttering about, the one that had been simmering in the immortal world for decades. It had not troubled him, not even the thought that his pack might perish in it.

But now he was ready to fight in this war, for her. With her. And they'd win it. Then he'd make sure she did not deny him again.

Chapter Four

"Let's start the killing now that I'm not dead, shall we?" Isla said with a grin, anger cutting through the energy in the clearing.

It was fair to say everyone was pretty ticked off. Isla had been pissed enough to rip Rick's arm off. Totally called for, in Sophie's opinion, since he'd tortured her and almost killed her. Granted, he didn't know she was in the grips of a spell that would make it so she didn't heal, but still, torture was a dick move.

She just wasn't that into him. Some men took rejection super badly.

Then again, there was apparently some kingly reason for the torture, but Sophie didn't buy it. Which was why she had almost stripped him of his mortality—something she didn't even know she'd been capable of until moments before—and likely destroyed herself by welcoming the power that simmered inside her.

Isla had saved the day by not dying.

Sophie sensed something else against the chill inside her while she was struggling to control her power.

Her wolf.

He was close.

But not close enough for anyone else to notice. Then again, Rick was distracted by his bleeding stump, Thorne was too busy making goo-goo eyes at Isla, Scott was recovering from her almost killing him, and Silver was glaring at her.

Still didn't accept the friend zone.

Sophie clapped. "Okay, well I've just realized I forgot to feed my cat, so I've got to go."

Isla frowned at her. "You don't have a cat."

"Well I've got to go and buy one, then," she snapped. "What self-respecting witch doesn't have a cat?"

"Easy—you," Isla said, crossing her arms. "You're not a self-respecting witch."

The presence moved closer. He'd be within scenting distance soon.

Sophie flipped Isla the bird. "Glad you're not dead, bloodsucker." She glared at Rick. "You got off easy. You'd do well to remember that in case you were thinking of fucking with my best friend again," she promised. "Walk it off, Scotty," she advised the dazed halfling. She pointedly ignored Silver. She didn't need that.

"Bye, losers."

And then she was gone, taking care to saunter for a hot minute, then run once she was out of sight.

The wolf ran with her. She waited for him to advance. To shout about the near-death experience, to fuck her against a tree trunk. Declare her his again.

He did none of these things.

To her utter dismay.

She waited for longer than she cared to admit, but he only remained at a distance, watching.

She bit her lip before she called out to him.

Then she stormed to her car.

The wolf was staying true to her wishes. She needed to stop

being such a fucking cliché female and start being the kickass witch she was.

Which meant it was time to fuck some shit up. Destroy the strongest—and evilest—witches known to man and monster.

And forget a particular monster.

༄

TWO DAYS Later

Calling spirits at a time like this was risky, to say the least, but she didn't have much of a choice, and if it wasn't a risk, it wasn't a party.

Plus, she needed a risk. She was bordering on desperate after the events at Thorne's place, and she'd found out nothing from all of her research.

It would be a good distraction from the fact that she hadn't seen hide nor hair of the wolf for days, only sensed him on occasion, but she could've been imagining that.

Sophie stood in front of the mirror, white candles covering every surface of her second bathroom—the first one was currently out of use on account of a great hulking fucking werewolf smashing a priceless vintage tub, which she still owed him a curse for—signifying the purity of the ritual.

Every candle color helped to fuel the magic to which they were connected, operating on a different frequency when lit by a witch. She technically should be surrounded by purple candles right now, if she wanted to follow the rules, which she never did. Purple connoted mystery, the strongest candle associated with astral travel and to connect a witch to unseen realms. Since she was trying to tap into the spiritual realm, it held to reason that purple was her jam.

And it was. She'd loved it because of its connection to mystery, power, and authority. Surrounding her apartment and work space in hues of purple candles helped to strengthen her connection with her physic self—one of the most important things for witches.

But she had gravitated to white this night. She told herself it was because she needed the added protection of its purity since her power was so closely connected to the grave she was looking to use as her physic telephone.

Not because of its connection with the lunar cycle.

With the *moon*.

Nope.

Her eyes reflected in the mirror swirled with flecks of silver and amber. A human might think it was a trick of the light. But of course, humans were idiots, and on the rare occasion they were paying enough attention to notice the magic that surrounded them, they came up with excuses for it, unable to reconcile the truth in their small brains.

"Terentia," Sophie called into the mirror, into the world beyond this one.

A candle flickered.

"On the realm of the spirits, I call for our Guardian," she continued, her voice having a musical quality to it she did not intend, brought upon by the power she was releasing. "I wish to convene on the space between our two worlds. On matters grave in knowledge and spirit. Come to the mirror in which I stand, I implore Terentia, our Guardian grand."

Sophie screwed up her nose at the unintended rhyme.

So lame.

But it worked. The mirror flickered like quicksilver, the chill of the grave grabbing at her like ice wind. The candles flickered once more, fighting off the evil spirits latching onto the death in Sophie's voice, aching to find purchase on her soul.

Her instincts had been right. Had she used purple, the conductor of the connection of realms, such spirits would've escaped the mirror and attacked Sophie.

"Child," the dim figure in the mirror called, coming to stark realness as if it was Sophie's own reflection.

The face was not beautiful and ethereal to match the voice. No flowing golden hair, radiant skin, majestic gown as many expected when they called on their first spirit.

This was a witch who now belonged to the underworld. Her beauty had been snatched away and given to those living.

Her skin was graying and decayed, peeling from her face, revealing chalky bones underneath. Lank yellow hair hung in clumps around the corpse's face, insects scuttering through the dirty strands.

She was naked, her skin peeling, rotting, and sagging all over her body, hanging off the bones that held her together.

Most young witches were terrified and traumatized on their first experience calling up one of the ancient witches. Sophie had not been. She wasn't even surprised. You were Facetiming a dead thing, what did you think you were going to be looking at? Kate Beckinsale?

She also found this ugly depiction of death beautiful in its truth, showing those living what a gift life really was. Death was ugly. More people—more witches—needed to realize this.

"Terentia," she replied, her voice thick with overarching respect the dead deserved. A lot more respect than the living.

Sophie's social niceties were more refined with corpses than anything else.

"Why have you called me from my rest?" Terentia asked, her voice gentle.

Spirits were not wrathful either. Well, some of them were. It depended on how they died, for sure, but mostly on what type of people—or immortals—they had been in their time on earth.

Basically, if you were an asshole in life, you'd be an even bigger asshole in death.

Terentia was a sacred Guardian to their kind, giving her life to save an entire coven of Wiccans. Not even real witches—in the magical sense of the word, anyway. They were just humans who tapped into the witch frequency and served with peace and love and all the bullshit Sophie despised.

But Terentia had loved them as servants of The Four, and given all her power to defeat the werewolves who had attacked their peaceful village centuries before.

She was kind of a kickass witch.

And she helped those sisters in need when it was a true and urgent matter. She wouldn't have appeared in the mirror otherwise.

"I need to know about the Herodias sisters," Sophie said. "They have escaped their bounds, and their spells have corrupted one who I care for." Sophie paused. "A sister." It wasn't exactly a lie —and you couldn't lie to a spirit—Isla was a sister to Sophie, the only one she had. Hopefully Terentia would assume this to be a sister witch, because no way in Hekate would she help a vampire.

Even saintly witches weren't going to help bloodsuckers.

Good thing Sophie wasn't a saintly witch.

Terentia's eyes swirled silver at her words, her grotesque face morphing in what Sophie guessed was alarm. It's not like there was a news channel in the otherworld, though she was surprised this was the first the spirits were hearing about it. Sophie's coven should've convened with them the moment the knowledge came to them.

Fishy.

"They have been freed?"

Sophie nodded. "Two have, from what I can gather. My sister defeated one, and the death spell weaved from Hades himself was her repayment. I need a way to counteract the spell."

Terentia watched Sophie for a long time. Well, at least it seemed like she was. It was pretty unnerving to have a dead witch zombie with silver eyes watch you through a mirror at first. But now Sophie had done it enough to know the dead witch zombie was combing through millennia of knowledge, both hers and the other witches who had perished in the name of The Four.

Knowledge did not die with the witch, in most cases. You just had to know which corpse to ask.

"You cannot counteract the spell," Terentia said finally.

Sophie sagged. She had a feeling that was going to be the case.

"To end the spell means to defeat the three dark ones. Not cage, but wipe them from this world and bar them from going to the next. True death is the only thing that can save your sister." That time the silver eyes were looking at Sophie, right into Sophie. And her skin froze at the look, the grave crawling over her like the insects in Terentia's hair. "And it is the only thing that will save you," the mirror witch whispered.

Fuck, she'd also had the feeling *that* was the case. Sophie had sensed the proximity of her own demise for years now.

"You need the grimoire," she continued. "You know where to seek it."

Sophie muttered a curse. Yes, she knew where to seek it, but that didn't mean she wanted to have to go and seek it herself. "I cannot conjure it?"

Terentia shook her head, a flap of her cheekbone moving in the breeze. "You know you cannot. It must be grasped with hands, not magic."

Sophie nodded once. "Thank you, Guardian. May your rest be peaceful and eternal."

It almost looked like the spirit smirked. "I doubt such a thing will be the case."

And then she was gone, all the candles flickering out and severing the connection with the underworld.

Good thing too. It was becoming too inviting.

She would've rather gone to the underworld at that point instead of the place she had to go to retrieve the book.

Her childhood home.

⁂

THE WOLF FOLLOWED HER.

Of course.

That time he showed himself to her.

It infuriated her, his constant presence. It infuriated her more that she felt comfortable, content in it too. That her entire body ached with need from the mere presence of his aura.

She knew his need existed too, because it was painted in every inch of his energy: her, the need for her, his devotion to her.

She had to ignore it. For whatever remaining sanity she had left.

"I thought I said I would end you if you came near me again," she hissed, slamming the door and shielding her hand from the sun to gaze up at the sprawling villa in front of them.

"You said I would meet Hades should I *force myself* on you," the wolf answered, surprising her. She hadn't expected him to speak, only to lurk. The wolf continued to surprise her. She hated that too. "I am not forcing myself," his gravelly voice continued. "I shall take you again only when you beg."

Her lady parts dipped at the pure sex in his tone.

Beg him right now, let him take you on the street.

She wasn't about to let her vagina talk for her. It had gotten her into enough trouble as it was.

"I'm here to do my duty," he continued.

She whipped her eyes from the decaying grandeur of her coven's home to the just plain grandeur of her wolf.

Fuck, you need to stop thinking of him as yours.

In the immortal words of Holly Golightly, people did not belong to people.

In this case, it was werewolves did not belong to witches, but the spirit still held true.

"And your duty is?" she asked with a hand on her hip.

His eyes went to that hand, where it was covering her exposed skin. She had dressed appropriately for her home visit, with a cropped tank that read 'Muggle in the sheets, witch in the sheets.'

She'd cut the bottom off it and showed half her tattooed midriff, and almost all of her aforementioned wild lady parts in a way low-slung ripped mini that barely covered her ass. She completed her look with thigh-high boots that laced all the way up.

She'd known her fellow estranged witches would hate it.

It seemed her wolf loved it.

Fuck.

"My duty," he ground out through an iron jaw, "is to protect my witch."

His words had her hackles rising, and she waved her hand to send him flying into the SUV he'd arrived in. He hit the roof with so much force he collapsed into the car, the smash ringing out on the deserted suburban street.

"In case you hadn't noticed, this witch doesn't need protecting," she hissed, turning on her heel. She clicked the locks of her Jeep. "But you might."

The door opened before she'd even walked up the wooden steps. The witches inside of the house obviously heard the crash and definitely felt the rush of magic that strictly wasn't meant to be practiced in broad daylight—despite the fact that this whole effing street was spelled to repel mortals.

She hid her flinch as she crossed the magic threshold designed to repel enemies; it smarted a little, as the spell couldn't decide whether she was friend or foe. She gave a slight magical push to get through it with both happiness and sadness at being recognized as foe.

Yes, they used to be her family. They'd raised her since birth, her parents having either died or abandoned her—there was some argument as to which, but no matter what, they'd left her. And the witches gave her a home, a resentment of authority and a tendency to overreact when people told her what to do. But they still raised her to be the fucked-up immortal she was, hence the sadness. But they were also Grade A bitches who wanted to control Sophie and grind down her spirit. Hence the happy part.

"Hey, I'm the black witch of the family," Sophie said with a finger wave at the shocked little witch who'd opened the door. "I've come for a cup of tea, maybe a scone and to snatch the oldest and most precious book of our kind. That cool?"

The witch was transfixed not by Sophie—which sucked, because Sophie considered herself rather transfixing, even on a bad eyeliner day—but at the wolf, who sounded like he'd extracted himself from the roof of the car and was likely coming toward the house.

Sophie waved in dismissal. "Oh, don't mind him. He's obsessed with me." She shrugged. "What can you do?"

Sophie gently shoved the teenage witch out of the doorway so she could step into the place she'd vowed she'd never return to. The smells and magicks rubbed over her skin like ragged wire, drawing blood from the emotional scars she'd been so sure had healed and then disappeared.

Nothing like going home again to show you how fucked up you pretended not to be.

There was a growl from the outside as Conall fought against the spell at the top of the stairs. She grinned. At least one thing was going to be fun—watching the wolf struggle.

She glanced back to the girl, who was most likely in her late teens, pretty, fresh-faced, naïve. Sophie gently probed her aura. The girl was powerful. Very powerful, if the not-so-gentle probe back was anything to go by.

Sophie grinned again. "Well, the kitten has claws," she observed. "Good for you. Make sure the stiffs here don't try to file them down or yank them from you for their own personal use. They've been known to do that." She winked.

Though she'd outwardly been focused on the young witch in front of her, she'd been prepared for the spell that was flung at her back, wiping it away with a quick counter spell as she turned.

She faced the three women responsible for her suffering and most likely responsible for this little witch's suffering—either past or present. It would happen. They liked to be the most powerful in the coven, and they weren't about to let the next generation change that.

"Spelling a girl while her back's turned?" Sophie tutted. "Now that's just bad form." Her eyes went up and down Hazel's slightly haggard appearance. "Not looking so hot, Haze," she teased. "Please tell me I have everything to do with that."

Weak bursts of fury cut through Hazel's aura. Nothing more bothersome than a gnat. She was juiced out after dealing with Sophie.

Sophie, on the other hand, was all riled up.

"You come into our sacred place, with a *wolf* of all things. You go too far, Sophie," Nora hissed.

Ah, so the heat at her back and the low growl was not a figment of her imagination. The wolf was right beside her, in the witch's den. She waved off the spells her former mentors shot at him.

"I know he's a dog and all that, but hitting him with spells that he can't even deflect is just plain *rude*," Sophie replied with a bored tone, though fury at their attacks boiled in her blood. "Where's your hospitality?"

Power circled around her and Conall as other witches in the coven joined the party. Some recognized Sophie, some did not. Some of them glared at her with hatred fueled by Hazel, Nora and

Morgan, some because she'd slept with their boyfriends and cursed them with acne when they pissed her off. None of them could match her power.

She was surprised to sense something else other than hatred from a handful of the witches. Something akin to... pride? Acceptance? Respect?

She couldn't pinpoint it because she'd never sensed it from fellow witches before. And distinguishing it from the unnatural and angry hate was rather hard.

Not the time to inspect it.

She focused on Nora, the boss bitch of the New York coven. She was outwardly beautiful, with a severe silver bob and lineless skin that contrasted with the age her hair color denoted. She was wearing earth tones, a brown sweater and darker brown corduroys —yes, you heard it—with chunky heeled boots peeking from below them. Crimes to the craft were not the only thing she committed. The fashion police really needed to lock her up.

Though she was beautiful, Sophie knew it was a glamor, her new powers seeing straight through it to the frizzed, waist-length hair, the liver spots, the crinkled skin. Love handles.

Sophie found herself wondering if she was always like that or if her sins against witchcraft had sucked away the almost eternal youth magic granted them.

It didn't really matter at that point. She had a book to steal and, as it happened, a werewolf to protect.

Despite her words, more pointed spells were directed at the snarling wolf. Though he hadn't changed yet, the air shimmered with his beast. Even the combined power of the coven would be no match for a turned werewolf. She hadn't seen him fully turned yet and she was curious. She was also tempted to let him rip them all to pieces.

But that wouldn't be very witchly of her.

She'd rather do it herself.

Anger rippled around her like a cape as she stepped in front of Conall and sent out a flare that blanketed the room in warning. The witches responsible for the attack all flinched in pain as Sophie's hits landed on their marks. "I said stop cursing the motherfucking wolf!" she yelled, her voice deepening and doubling like she had some kind of Darth Vader mask on.

Silence stretched through the room after her words. Nora even looked shocked.

Sophie smiled placidly. "Now," she said in a more even tone, "can we not all just get along?"

Nora recovered quickly. "We will not accept a witch who does not align herself with the coven's interest, Sophie," she spat. "You have betrayed every one of us. Unless you listen to your elders and rectify your ways, we are forced to take action." Threat punctured every one of the words, and once again, Conall growled.

Sophie rolled her eyes. "I'm the one doing the protecting here, wolf, remember? You just stand there and be quiet. Use a piece of furniture as a chew toy if you must." She pointed to the patterned antique sofa in the corner. "Go wild. I've always hated that."

Her focus moved to the three witches in front of her.

"Sorry, you don't tell me how to be a witch," she snapped. "If I wanted a dictatorship, I'd go to China. Or church. So I'm going to have to take a hard no on the whole 'toe the line or we'll lock you up' thing you've got going on." Sophie stepped forward, calling upon the magic she knew they'd be terrified by. To be fair, it terrified her too. "You think *I've* spattered our legacy? No, that's you. You've disrespected the freedoms granted to us by The Four in order to bastardize our gift and try to make it a power you can wield." She smiled again as she knocked away a strike with the wave of her hand. Conall growled at the attack, baring his teeth aggressively. She ignored this too.

"What was brought down upon me, be it returned times three," she began to chant, her words weaving through the air, paralyzing the coven that was trying to use the powers of her bloodline against her. "Head to toe, skin and nerve, may you get exactly what you deserve." The spell spun through the air like a mini tornado, sucking up every inch of bad intention that had been brought against her and hurling it toward her enemies.

Enemies she used to consider sisters.

But not anymore.

Sophie ignored this pang.

"I'm not a huge fan of spells that rhyme," she said lightly. "I usually find them so... *tacky*." She screwed up her nose. "But on this occasion, I'll make an exception, since it's likely to be so very effective."

Then she turned on her heel and left karma and a little bit of magic—okay, a whole lotta magic—to do its worst.

The wolf followed her in her descent down the stairs, the crashes and shrieks from above calming Sophie. She'd done nothing deadly or permanent—to her great disappointment—just created enough disorder to make sure she got what she came for without any more drama.

The rooms below ground were almost as sprawling as the house itself. They contained ancient relics, herbs, countless grimoires, and the odd cage or two, for when a witch misbehaved.

Sophie touched the bars of the middle one, grinning at where she'd carved her name and left lewd drawings. "Ah, the teenage years," she muttered.

Again she ignored the pure rage emanating from Conall at his realization that she used to hang out in those bars.

"Chill, wolf," she said, sauntering into the bowels of the basement, flicking the locks open with a small spell. "It's not like I'm a stranger to a jail cell. It actually really helped me during my first drunk and disorderly." She turned and winked. Then she put her attention on the book in the middle of the room.

It was the only thing in the room, sitting atop a large wooden table. The air was heavy in there, damp and vibrating with power from the oldest and most sacred books of her coven. She flinched as the power stung her skin. Her head whipped around again, to the wolf about to follow her into the room.

"Stop!" she yelled, with a little more desperation than she intended. It worked though because the wolf froze. She pushed him safely out of the doorway with a spell.

He growled at that, eyes wide in accusation.

"Beings without magic cannot venture in here," she said. "Unless they want to die a really shitty death." She paused. "But come right ahead if that means it'll stop you following me."

The wolf looked from her to the room, as if he was tasting the truth in her words. He splayed his feet and crossed his arms, cementing himself in place. So he was going to listen to her, but not go anywhere. Awesome.

"Okay, whatever, I thought you lived to protect my happiness," she muttered, turning to face the book.

It had been strictly forbidden to venture in there as a child, so naturally she crept in every other day. She had only ever gotten to touch the front of the ancient book before she was caught and thrown in a cell for a witch version of time-out. But the sheer power and knowledge that came from the simple touch intoxicated and terrified a young Sophie. She'd sensed it then, even when her powers were still growing, that there was a responsibility that came to anyone who opened that book.

So naturally she stopped trying to read it. She wanted responsibility like she wanted to share an elevator with Justin Bieber. In other words, not on her life.

But there she was, grabbing the book that would well and truly make her a witch grownup. Her hand hovered across the pentagram carved into the leather of the book.

She almost left, walked right out and let someone else be the one to have to deal with whatever magical worms jumped out of the proverbial can.

But then she thought of Isla, of the memory of her almost dying, of the death that still clung to her aura. Without blinking, she snatched the book and strode out, breezing past the wolf as she did so.

And so it begins.

Chapter Five

❧

"You're not riding with me," Sophie hissed as the werewolf opened the passenger door.

He glanced back to the ruined SUV, obviously undriveable.

"That's not on me," she said. "You chose to follow me. You should've expected your form of transportation to be ruined." She paused. "Just be glad it wasn't your legs." She placed the grimoire on the passenger seat when she sensed he was about to ignore her.

He stalled immediately; even a wolf could sense the power coming from it.

"You sit on that, see what happens," she invited. "Or better yet, try to move it. I dare you."

He did not move.

Sophie grinned. "Yeah, didn't think so." She glanced to the house, which was now quiet. "Ah, perfect timing. For once, the witches are going to help me by ensuring my tail, who coincidently *has a tail*, is too distracted by their magical murder attempts to follow me." She shoved him back with a spell once more, using the last of her strength. She was pretty close to tapped out right now.

"Toodles." She finger-waved and screeched off, the door slamming shut with the force of her acceleration.

She glanced in the rearview mirror as he growled and made to give chase, but a swift spell by Nora nipped that in the bud.

She felt a pang of something akin to guilt mingled with worry. She shook it off. The witches wouldn't actually be able to kill her wolf—he was much too strong for that. They would merely slow him down and ensure that he wasn't sitting in an enclosed space with her.

She would not have survived the car ride back into the city with him right next to her. She would've pulled over and begged him to take her right there and then, ancient grimoire, death spells, and ancient evil be damned.

Destruction was already all around, and she was fighting it. The last thing she needed to be doing was beg for it.

She glanced at the book that seemed to be staring at her.

A strong premonition seized her. This was the end of life as she knew it.

She gritted her teeth and focused on the road.

"Tell me something I don't know," she muttered.

SHE OBVIOUSLY DIDN'T GO home, because that would've been the first place the wolf would look. And because he'd already ruined her elevator, her dining room table—okay, that was Hazel—her curtains—that may have been her—and her bed.

Luckily she had her office. Though that had taken a beating lately too, when slayers and evil vampires had burst into it to steal the human turned vampire Frankenstein Sophie had captured.

It had been an eventful year.

Luckily she had an amazing contractor who she may have put

the tiniest spell on to ensure he worked faster and more efficiently. How else were you meant to get a contractor to show up on time?

The second she'd opened the book, it had yanked her in, as if hands had emerged from the pages, taken hold of her brain and imprinted it in the pages.

There was no other explanation for the reason why, when she glanced up seconds later, the midday sun shone through the windows of her office when it was the waxing moon shining through seconds before.

She glanced at the clock, took stock of her near-exploding bladder and screaming hungry stomach.

"Shit," she muttered. "This book is legit."

She glanced down at the runes covering the aged paper. All written in a dead language that Sophie couldn't even freaking *read*, but somehow the entire book was burned into her brain, as if she'd memorized it.

That was either extremely good or extremely bad.

That was something for another time. Sophie needed coffee, shower, and a cheeseburger.

Evil could wait.

Werewolves, apparently, could not.

˚

Fighting the witches off had taken much of his strength. Especially when he'd had to make the effort not to kill them.

He had ached to do so because of their violence toward Sophie, the obvious hurt they'd caused her.

That cage in the bowels of the sweet and foul-smelling house was burned into his brain. They had put her there.

As a *child*.

Even his clan were not as brutal to their young.

My former clan, he corrected himself.

Ugly, brutal, and evil they might be, but they were her kin. She deserved to exact her own vengeance over them as she saw fit. Plus there were young there who had no part in this war yet. He would not spill their blood.

The silver-haired witch with the double face, on the other hand, he had to battle not to rip her throat out. But he did not. And it always took more strength to spare a foe than it did to kill them.

Then he'd had to run much of the way into the city before he could find a car to steal. His body had required nourishment, yet another thing to slow him down. But likely when he found his witch, he'd find her in trouble, so he needed his strength to protect her.

Not that she needed protecting.

He was quickly learning that.

In the witches' manor, she'd stood in front of him, using her magic as a shield against her own kin and then as a sword to avenge him.

That should have ground against his nature, a female doing the protecting that was reserved for him.

It did not. It made him proud. His witch was a warrior.

But that did not mean she did not need help. In the days since he'd made his vow to protect her until she begged to be claimed, Conall had felled at least a dozen assassins lying in wait for his witch.

Vampires, demons, even wolves. He hadn't given any of them mercy nor escape. Cold recognition had painted the faces of the wolves who'd glimpsed him in his true form.

"It can't be," one of them had uttered.

But then he'd uttered no more because Conall ripped his heart out.

Sophie was a target for the rebels mounting an assault against all established immortal leadership.

How she was in the middle of such a thing, Conall did not know. She was powerful, yes. And had a smart mouth that would likely piss a lot of immortals off and harden their cocks at the same time. But even his witch didn't have a smart enough mouth to make her one of the top targets in the biggest war he had seen in his time on earth.

And that book had sent his hackles up, the wolf inside him telling him it housed great power. Not necessarily evil, but something that could be molded to be whatever a powerful sorcerer wanted.

A weapon in the right hands.

And Sophie had it in *her fucking hands*. She had been spent when she'd driven off; he'd scented it on her, the waning strength.

So she was weakened, walking around with a weapon that the rebellion would kill for, already on their list of targets and he didn't fucking know why.

Never had he cursed his forced solitary existence until now. His desperation was almost wild enough to do something he'd vowed never to do while he drew breath: contact his clan for information.

The thought curdled the food in his stomach as he prowled the rancid city searching for her scent. But he vowed to himself that he would do it if he did not find her soon.

He had heard she was some kind of investigator, some kind of mercenary, and it had taken him longer than he liked to locate her offices. He scented her three blocks away.

She was there.

And she was going to be sorry.

§⁂

LUCKILY, Sophie had a rudimentary apartment upstairs, since she owned the whole building—being a mercenary was profitable, and she'd mastered spells to manipulate the stock market. Highly against the witch code of ethics.

Hey, a witch couldn't be perfect, but she could be rich.

Once she'd gotten herself caffeinated and somewhat fed on some Lucky Charms she kept in case of emergency, she showered.

The hot water was heaven on her taut muscles, screaming out from the time spent in the same position. She could scant believe it, but there were few things impossible in the magical world, so she just accepted it.

There was no point in dwelling on how she read an ancient book in a dead language she didn't know, or how she lost twelve hours of her life doing so. It was more important to utilize what she'd learned.

The true story of how Malena and her sisters, Belladonna and Ucillia, gained their dark power by subverting the most sacred of the witches' laws. By twisting the natural and pure power given to them by nature herself and tarnishing it with evil and death.

One thing that had irked Sophie more than that, than their obvious, almost indestructible power, were the similarities she drew with Malena.

She was a witch, a powerful one, who hated being told what to do and eventually rebelled.

Granted, Sophie had never turned a bunch of humans into vampire hybrids, intent on creating an army to enslave humanity, but one time she did enchant a whole One Direction concert to be completely silent and not move for twenty minutes.

Plus, Malena had partnered with the king of Hell for that little jaunt, whereas Isla had been Sophie's partner in crime. Not quite a Hades level of evil, though some people might disagree with her there.

But the council had executed her sisters for her crimes, not just Malena herself—that's how deep their sickening need for power went, to the point where it endangered everything The Four had gifted witches, and now their choice was pretty close to ending life on earth as they knew it.

Plus, they'd locked Sophie up for ten days while The Sex Pistols were touring. The council had caused all the havoc those thousands of years ago, and it wasn't even them who cleaned it up. They shifted blame better than the current president.

"And the Herodias sisters were banished to the cave, which was neither in the space of living nor dead, since their crimes to both life and death meant they would never embrace the reaper for the stillness of death, nor ever taste the beautiful chaos of life. Forever bound, or shall the earth be tainted and ruined should the chains of their prison be broken."

Sophie shivered under the hot spray of the shower, the words of the book burned into her brain. Not just because they felt like a harbinger of doom, but because it wasn't the Herodias sisters she saw being trapped in the mid-world between life and death, it was her.

If she didn't find a way to understand and control her power.

But there just wasn't time.

Between assassination attempts, her best friend's looming death the wolf who wanted to mate her, her day job, and listening to the latest Thirty Seconds to Mars album.

Her Jared Leto thoughts were cut short when the shower curtain screeched open and a wolf stood in front of her.

She raised her brow, congratulating herself for not flinching or even letting out the little scream she caught in her throat.

Sophie had been caught by surprise enough times to master a poker face, though the beings who usually caught her had murder in their eyes, not lust. To be fair, there was a fair bit of murder too. She guessed the wolf was none too happy about being left with a coven of pissed-off witches.

"I'm trying to shower here," she said blandly, making every effort to keep her voice even and not husky with the desire she felt with the heat of his gaze.

He let out a growl. "This is all you have to say for yourself?"

She shrugged, and the motion meant his gaze was wrenched from her eyes to her breasts. Her nipples immediately hardened as the beast took over his eyes, lighting them pure gold.

He stepped into the small shower cubicle under the spray and she backed herself into the wall, his arms framing either side of her shoulders, boxing her in as the water cascaded over him, over his clothes, his boots.

The wolf didn't seem to notice.

It was as if he wouldn't notice if a plane crashed in the next room. Sophie doubted she would either.

"You're going to beg now," he growled, making sure not to touch her, other than the hot air radiating from him that had nothing to do with the steam from the shower.

Sophie blinked up at him, her knees quivering, heart smashing against her ribs.

Do it! Her vagina screamed. *Get on your knees and beg, then give him the best BJ of his life to apologize for siccing a coven of witches on him.*

Sophie hated that she leaned forward, catching herself before she did exactly what every cell in her body, every organ it seemed, was screaming her to do.

"I will never beg," she hissed, jutting out her chin and holding onto her history to remind her how matters of the heart ended.

In death.

And she sensed this would be one she couldn't come back from.

When did this stop being about the vagina and start being about the heart?

His jaw was granite and his face shimmered with the force of the beast inside him willing a change, battling for control. It had to hurt, Sophie knew. In fact, she could feel the pain as his bones protested, as his desire choked at him to do the one thing the animal inside him willed him to do.

Claim.

The secondhand pain was even difficult to bear.

But he did.

For her.

She ignored whatever feelings she had at that. She had to.

His golden irises moved down her body slowly, in direct conflict with the chaos in his eyes. They traced her collarbone as forcefully as his large callused hands might. Then they moved, circling her nipple in a gaze so intense that Sophie audibly gasped.

If her eyes had not been glued to him, she would've sworn he'd touched her, tweaked her nipple, suckled it. But his hands stayed at either side of her head, caging her in.

Her thighs throbbed with need and her breath became shallower as he steadily moved his eyes downward, past the droplets of water snaking past her belly button, over the ridges of her hips.

"Wolf," she gasped as his eyes focused on her core with a force that must have been supernatural. His mere gaze was edging her toward climax.

That was impossible.

Didn't you just think about the fact that nothing was impossible? the rational witch inside her asked. She never got much stage time.

"Beg," he growled again, his voice a caress and a whip at the same time. His eyes were still on her pussy, as if they were devouring her. He licked his lips.

Sophie struggled to stay upright, to not wrap her legs around his waist and ride the hard length pressing against his jeans.

But that would mean you give in. You surrender. That would mean he owns you.

She ripped her eyes upward. "No." She ground the word out with physical pain.

Again the beast ripped at his irises, his body as tight as a nocked bow. She thought for a delicious moment that he might break his word, that he might yank her to him and devour her like the wolf in the story, destroy her.

Parts of her ached for that.

But he stepped back.

"You will," he promised.

And then he left.

Then he fucking *left*.

Chapter Six

"Do you have a death wish?" Sophie demanded, whirling on the wolf the second she sensed his presence.

She got the idea that he'd been following her the entire time and she was only just realizing it, and that pissed her right off.

They were in the strangely deserted alley outside Dante's Inferno. Not the book, the bar. Run by a demon. True story.

"Do you?" he demanded, fury injected into his voice, his eyes pointedly going to the bar behind them.

"Not today," she snapped. "I'm meeting my bestie for a drink, not that the werewolf who's about to be smote off the face of the earth needs that information to pass on to Hades, since I'm sure he knows already. He keeps dibs on Isla. His most coveted soul. If she has one."

Conall did not seem to appreciate her tirade, which was fitting, since she didn't appreciate his... everything.

Well that was a total lie, since she infuriatingly appreciated everything about him. He'd obviously changed out of his drenched clothes after he'd left her naked and wanting in the shower. He'd trimmed his stubble slightly, but his hair was still beautifully wild.

"This is not just a drink," he ground out.

She tilted her head. "And I agree to disagree." He wasn't to know that nine out of ten times she and Isla had a 'drink,' it ended in some kind of battle. Or explosion. Or small civil war. "And you can keep playing with your own demise by following me, wolf."

Then she turned on her booted foot before she did something incredibly stupid like run up to him and kiss the life out of him instead of stamping the life out of him as she should've.

🕯

He followed her into the bar, every inch of his body radiating in fury. His entire being screamed at him to snatch her, with force if need be, and take her away from danger. Because he knew blood would be spilled that night. His beast could sense it. And was hungry for it.

Sophie seemed to be hungry for it too.

And he was hungry for her.

Leaving her wet, naked, and near mad with desire hours before had been hands down the hardest thing he'd ever had to do.

The entire afternoon was spent trying to sate his need with his hand. Then, when that didn't work, he'd hunted a cluster of demons.

Tearing them limb from limb hadn't helped him at all. He was worried he might tip over into insanity if he didn't have her soon. Only one memory of being inside her was worse than having none, because he knew how perfect his woman was, how it felt to have her milk his orgasm from his body. And that was worse than anything his imagination could conjure up.

But he would not force her, not even when her eyes and body begged for it. Only when her words did.

He might yet go insane, but rather that than hurt his mate.

So that was why he sat there in the corner all night, not moving a muscle as demons, vampires, warlocks, and every other kind of creature frequenting the bar tried to hit on what was there.

Tried being the operative word. And the only reason he'd stayed seated.

Every single immortal who sauntered up to his witch either got turned around with a confused look on their face, as if they didn't remember their own name, or doubled over in pain.

That pleased him.

Then there was the redheaded vampire who sauntered in, battling a demon on entrance after declaring her coupling with a Praseates.

Daring, and almost suicidal.

Definitely crazy.

Dangerous.

So obviously she was Sophie's friend.

He clenched his fists against the table, cutting into his palms as his claws extended.

Even he had encountered the infamous she-vampire. She was as mad as she was strong, legendary in battle, and known for causing more trouble to both the mortal and immortal worlds than any other creature on this earth.

Hades himself included.

The demon the vampire had punched was writhing on the floor. She regarded him as little more than a doorstop as she glanced up at Conall's mate, drinking a cocktail with an umbrella sticking out of it of all things, looking bored. Like she'd seen this before.

My warrior.

"Cute boots," the vampire noted.

Sophie glanced down, extending her long leg so she—and every hot- and cold-blooded male in the bar—could see it. Her beautiful face scrunched up. "Thanks. They're new. I was wondering if they went with this outfit."

Conall's claws cut into the wood.

Outfit.

Was that what she called it?

His mate showed a lot of skin. So much so it caused him to near decapitate anyone who glanced her way—which was everyone. He might like it, if she had been properly claimed by him, so everyone would *see* what was his, but everyone most certainly couldn't fucking *touch*.

As it was, she wasn't claimed by him, hence the homicidal thoughts at every new torture device designed to taunt him with her perfect body.

That night it was a black sheathe that barely covered her peach ass and molded to every one of her sinful curves.

Conall's shaft throbbed painfully.

The boots in question were thigh high, only showing a sliver of skin despite the dress's lack of coverage. It only made her look more naked somehow. And Conall more crazed.

There had been further conversation about the boots, like they were in a Macy's instead of a bar with an incapacitated demon bleeding everywhere.

The vampire was grinning with a look of pure madness. *She* was where Sophie fit into this rebellion. He was sure of it. She was the reason his mate was in danger.

His immediate instinct was to end her. Right now.

But they were friends. Such an action would hurt Sophie and likely make sure he lost her forever.

"Oh, can you do some mojo to make sure his healing is at the rate of a human?" the vampire asked Sophie conversationally. "Or even a… I don't know, what heals slower than a human?" she mused while twisting her heel into the demon's rib cage.

Both she and Sophie acted like this was nothing.

Sophie scrunched her nose with an adorable edge that did not betray the fact that they were talking about the torture and potential death of a demon. Not that Conall liked them. He despised them, in fact. He'd just never encountered such women. They were more bloodthirsty than even wolf females.

Which was why he hadn't been mated with one. Not bloodthirsty enough. He'd thought his mate would be calmer, to tame him, but now he knew she had to be even wilder than him so they could embrace chaos together.

"Not much," Sophie answered the vampire's question. "Human it is."

Immediately the scent of her magic enveloped him. It was a homing beacon to him now; he'd recognize it even when surrounded by other spellcasters. It was sweet, intoxicating, with a hint of menace that both excited and terrified him.

Because it was yet to be determined whether the menace would control Sophie or she would control it.

"Thanks," the vampire said once the spell was done.

Sophie was studiously ignoring him, but even now he scented her desire for him.

She raised her glass to the vampire. "Anytime."

If that was how their 'drinks' began, Conall hated to think how the rest of the night would go.

How many deaths would add up to be given to Hades?

He didn't much care.

One thing he was certain of was that it wouldn't be his mate's.

⁂

THE DEATH BEGAN QUICKER than anticipated, nowhere near the end of the night. Conall had been so concentrated on listening to the conversations of witches and curses and Russia, he had not scented the enemies until they had burst through the doors of the bar.

Obviously their target was Sophie.

He was across his table and ripping the throat of a demon out in less than a second.

The vampire reacted just as quickly, blocking a werewolf in mid-transition from coming near Sophie. Conall roared at the danger, half changing so he could take down a vampire with its fangs extended.

Sophie's magic blanketed the air as he ripped through his foes to get to her, save her.

But she was not in need of saving. No. Her hair fluttered in the wind though there was no breeze that night. Her palms were cyan blue and her eyes were glowing.

Fucking *glowing*.

And every single attacker who even veered toward her toppled to the ground. Some without their heads. All of them dead.

He didn't have time to marvel at her magnificence. Even with her power, the vampire's fighting skill, and the demon behind the bar, there were more enemies than perhaps they could handle.

No! the beast roared. His mate would not perish. Not that night.

He tore at enemies with a ferocity that he didn't realize he was capable of without changing completely. Vampires tore at his skin, demons broke bones, but none of it slowed him, nor even gave him pause.

The air was thick around Sophie, sweet and sour as she dealt death like she controlled the deadliest blackjack known to immortals—and the house always won. The redheaded vampire tore into the growing mob with more viciousness and strength than he'd seen from some of his fiercest warriors.

She hadn't blinked when a horned demon—not wearing a human form, almost unheard of—started for her. He knew that most immortals—most *smart* immortals—would've known that death was certain and would've run. Demons in their true forms were stronger than most turned wolves.

But the vampire was either stronger than most, stubborner than most, or more stupid.

He reasoned it was a combination of all three when the demon threw her across the room and Conall caught her, setting her on her feet as he saw her chest bone jutting outward. A nasty wound, even for a vampire. He scented death on her.

His need to protect Sophie yanked at his gaze as she was quickly surrounded by attackers. She was fighting them off, but he would not let her do it alone. Though the vampire would likely die without his help, and though he hated them, this particular one was the only friend he had seen Sophie with, and after the scene with the witches, he knew she needed friends—strong ones.

The vampire must have sensed that, as she grinned up at him. Grinned amongst the death and destruction around them and within her.

He was wrong—she was not strong, stubborn, or stupid.

She was just insane.

"Chill, Cujo. I've got this one," she said, winking. Her eyes went to Sophie, whose own irises were glowing as the air became bitter with a more dangerous magic. His beast roared at him. She was in more danger from what was within her than every immortal in this room.

The vampire's eyes were grim. "Go and make sure the magic inside Sophie doesn't have her head twisting all types of ways, won't you? We've got enough excitement for tonight."

She stepped back toward the demon that would likely kill her, and Conall's beast took control as he sprinted toward his mate.

Toward the witch who was quickly replacing his mate.

Bodies piled up around him as he snatched immortal's out of the air with renewed speed, renewed urgency. He knew he had little time before the bitter magic snatched Sophie from his grasp.

His muscles burned when he ripped the head off the last demon in front of her.

Then he wasn't moving, magic cementing his blood, his very breath.

She stepped in front of him, face rippling, almost turning with the force of the magic battling to take control. But she was still there. He could sense her.

"*La mia luna*," he gritted out, though the words were razors at his throat.

Pain electrified every cell in his body as she tried to will him to his knees. He did not do so, the beast in him pushing forward so he broke free enough to grasp the sides of her face. His palms burned on contact, as if he'd dipped them into an inferno, but he did not let go.

"You do not leave this world, *luna mia*," he commanded, his voice rippling into a growl. "I command you not to. And you must come back to me in order to yell at me for commanding such things."

She blinked. More of her violet came back into the silver eyes.

"You still have to beg me, remember?" he continued, his voice near feral.

Another blink.

The air started to become sweeter as the foulness of the power receded and Sophie's eyes cleared even more.

She didn't even skip a beat as they narrowed at him. "Why do you insist on trying to save the day when I've got it the fuck covered?" she snapped, voice sharp but he could hear the slight shake in it.

The tightly coiled fear that had wrapped around his heart loosened some, and he gained enough power over his limbs to release her face and yank her small, shaking body into his arms. He expected her to struggle—she was his little warrior, after all—but she sank into him. That small relaxing of her body chased away every inch of pain that had pulsated through his own.

Of course, it didn't last.

"Holy James Franco!" she yelled, pushing him away from her and sprinting to the door. She leapt over the bodies surrounding her with the grace of a gymnast, one who'd done such a thing before.

The corpse of the demon flew through a window with the swipe of her hand.

In tune with every part of her energy, he knew his mate had used up almost the last of it coming back from the edge.

"Isla, you bitch," she hissed, sinking down to her knees beside the body of her vampire. "I told you no more dying. We have backstage passes to Thirty Seconds to Mars next month."

Sharp and real pain stabbed at his stomach, secondhand from Sophie. It leeched into her tone.

He decided at that moment that, if the vampire wasn't lost already, he'd do anything and everything within his power to make sure the insane redhead stayed alive. If only so his mate didn't have to feel an ounce more of that pain, that loss.

THEY ENDED up in Sophie's offices. This was after Sophie had used the very last of her strength to try to heal her lifeless friend. He'd felt it seeping out of her, her very life force. She was literally clawing at the last snatches of what she had left in order to give a vampire—one who was technically already dead—life.

"*La mia luna*," he murmured, holding himself back from snatching at her neck and yanking her away from the vampire. He wanted to. By fuck he wanted to. Standing there and watching his mate almost kill herself trying to heal a bloodsucker was scraping against his insides. His beast roared at him to do *anything* to rip Sophie away from the grave she was falling into.

But he knew that would be a mistake.

So he held back.

"Not now, wolf." Her voice was flat, losing vibrancy.

He placed his hand lightly on the back of her neck, laying his lips on her head, wishing he could have her sorcery in order to give her every ounce of his own strength.

"It is not working," he said gently, voice tight. "You know that magic is not what she needs."

Her body was worried. "You don't know what she needs," she hissed, voice broken. "You don't know what I can do." That time her voice turned, becoming unfamiliar, and Conall's body froze at the bitter magic creeping into the air. Into his bones.

Death magic.

He forced himself to calm, using his hold on Sophie's neck as an anchor. "She does not need her friend to kill herself, or damn herself. I know this," he growled. He held himself back from saying he did not need that. He would not live with that. This wasn't about him.

His grip tightened as the air became thicker with the hold of death Sophie was calling on to try to bring about life.

"Isla," a rough voice demanded.

Conall barely acknowledged the demon who was rushing through the corpses. He had fought with them. He was not a threat.

As if Sophie's magic was a wall, the demon stopped when he first encountered it, eyes wild, looking from the lifeless vampire to the death-saturated witch.

"*La mia luna,*" he continued, giving the demon a meaningful look to stay back. For now. If Sophie did not listen, he may need the help of the demon to take her out.

But he feared even both of them would not be enough.

"She needs blood," he gritted out. "*Life*. She does not need you to call on death. You know that."

The silence after his words hung in the air like daggers above their heads, waiting.

It was a tight moment, between destruction and resurrection—just not the kind Sophie was calling on.

Then, like a tide, the invisible black tar in the air receded. Sophie's sweet energy rushed in to replace it, and he let out the first breath he'd taken in minutes.

He squeezed her neck again.

She shook out of his grasp, standing on shaky feet. Her eyes went to the demon. "Well, don't just stand there," she snapped. "Use those muscles, pick the vampire the fuck up and let's go find a human for her to snack on."

The demon jumped to heed her command, maybe because of the residual fear in his eyes after seeing her true power, maybe because of the true panic at seeing the unresponsive vampire.

Sophie glanced to Conall, face drawn, body painted in exhaustion, but fire burned in her eyes.

My warrior.

"I don't suppose you drove here?" she questioned.

He shook his head once.

"Damn," she cursed. "Well, that demon better run fast."

And without a second to snatch her into his arms, taste the life on her skin, remind himself that she was not lost—yet—she was vaulting over the bodies with an urgency that trumped her exhaustion.

The demon was already halfway down the alley when a van screeched in front of it. Conall reached around and threw Sophie behind him, calling on the beast, preparing for a threat.

Though it was a smiling vampire with an eye patch who emerged from the van. First he was grinning with the innocence of youth that Conall didn't think existed anymore, but then his eyes touched on the vampire in the demon's arms.

"Stop pushing me behind you, asshole," Sophie snapped, punching him in the shoulder with her tiny fist and stomping to the frozen vampire. "Scotty, don't stare. Isla would not appreciate you having such an unflattering image of her in your mind. Get in the van and fucking *drive*."

He didn't hesitate.

Neither had the demon.

So obviously neither did Conall.

Sophie's dread saturated his skin and he ached to do something, but he was helpless.

He despised that.

More so when the blood the vampire was given spewed out of her along with whatever life was lingering in her cold body. Sophie's panic and dread nearly choked him then. He didn't understand her cool demeanor, her strict and firm orders under such emotion, but he was proud as fuck of her. At her strength.

It was magic not gifted to her. It was *her*. Sophie.

And it paid off. The vampire recovered with a sarcastic quip that he was coming to see was characteristic. He would've been angered at such a flippant disregard for her life and Sophie's pain, but he'd seen her fight. Seen her concern for Sophie in the battle. She would die for his witch.

So that was how they wound up in Sophie's offices. How he was surrounded by vampires. It should have made his skin crawl, their proximity. It did not. Sophie was there. That was it.

But he sensed there was something coming in this small room with an unlikely assortment of immortals.

Something that brought death. Something that lived inside his mate.

It was wrapped up around her core, her being. Especially when that book, the one radiating ancient power, entered the conversation.

He knew everyone in the room sensed its power, saw the way even the king of vampires—who had arrived soon after they had entered Sophie's office— tensed when Sophie presented it.

Even the redheaded vampire spouting sarcastic remarks knew it was something to be feared.

"Witches are born of the earth, from the soul of nature itself." Sophie's musical voice silenced all chatter, mingled with the dread she'd introduced when talking of the Herodias sisters. Even Conall had heard of them. His father was among the immortals who fought to banish them in a cave.

It had cost his clan a lot, that fight. Those witches. Ended up costing Conall everything. So his heart had filled with poison at the mention of them in proximity to the one being on this earth he treasured.

His witch continued, unware of his anxiety. "God bestowed power over the first mortal women to gain the powers of the elements. Not like the vampires or the werewolves." Her eyes touched his, warming him with her gaze, with their connection.

It was too fleeting before she continued to talk of the powers of witches.

"It was neither good nor evil, what The Four were blessed with, just power itself," she said, her voice husky and low. Conall's cock twitched at the depth of it. He needed her. "But it is dangerous, that neutrality, especially when put into human spirits. Which is why the most ancient of us created the rules that bind every witch, that forbid the use of natural powers for unnatural acts. Because it's there. The power."

Her words brought about the cold breeze of the past as Conall was thrust into the memory of what the air had tasted like in the bar. That was what she was talking about. A power that craved a hold. A vessel.

That was inside her.

He was swimming, drowning in the thought of losing her when he snapped himself out of it to listen. He needed this information. Information his mate had not given him freely.

She would be sorry for that.

His cock twitched again.

Her gaze was focused on the vampire as Sophie nodded at something she said. "The council has not changed, for their pursuit of power and the witches who wield it stains the blood of this book, even if one can't see it," she said, her voice hard and soft at the same time.

Conall's instincts screamed at him with a strange dread at those words. Something yanking at his bond with his witch. Something intent on taking her away.

He glanced at the vampire. He had no love for the redheaded bloodsucker, but he saw the determination in her eyes to eliminate anyone who threatened his witch.

Sophie continued to tell the story of the witch sisters. Conall listened, but he also started to plan the demise of this council.

He would end them all.

He would enjoy it.

"And the Herodias sisters were banished to the cave, which was neither in the space of living nor dead, since their crimes to both life and death meant they would never embrace the reaper for the stillness of death, nor ever taste the beautiful chaos of life." Sophie's words wound around him like a terrible melody. "Forever bound, or shall the earth be tainted and ruined should the chains of their prison be broken."

Again his past was hurled at him. His life before Sophie, before the wasteland of his solitary existence. The time when he belonged to a clan. When his clan followed him through the moonlight.

He dug his claws into the palms of his hands to chase away those memories. To chase away the rage at the witches for setting a course of events that would ruin his life.

But then had it not been in a ruined life that he had found his mate?

Did he not have these witches to thank for finding his mate?

Yes, he would thank them. Then he would tear them to pieces.

Something entered the air and Conall's hackles rose, his body tightened against the threat.

"It is because the two have returned that the blood shall not be sullied with anything but the design of the gods should the world hope to flourish in a new age of peace."

Conall searched for the source of the foreign voice until he realized it was fucking Sophie. Something coming from inside her.

His claws dug farther into his palms as he used the pain to keep him in place. To stop him from clutching Sophie tightly, shaking her back to herself. That would not work. The emptiness in her eyes told him as much. He could not bring her back. He would wait. He had to.

His eyes didn't move from his statuesque witch as the vampire argued with her human. Sophie didn't even fucking *breathe*. Blink.

"She will be deathless, this chosen one." Her voice fluttered through the air, iron in Conall's lungs.

"The one like the one who came first before her," the eerie voice continued. "First before her, but was the one who submitted to the mortality she was plagued with. Her head of fire in the sky for all to see, the emerald of her eyes in the oceans which glint from the sunlight that banished her mate to the darkness until it was no longer the place where monsters lurked. For the light was their home more than the shadows."

Conall's beast roared against his chest, against his ribs. But he stayed still.

"In the shadows and in the light, they come back. Come back with the chosen one. Deathless until the blood of her mate is drained or ash if the heart stops beating. Then her death shall come swift and fast, and on the heels of this, the end of the world."

The silence after her words was a resounding roar so loud he barely heard the vampire's response to Sophie's words.

No, not *Sophie's* words.

He shook as she rubbed at her head, her eyes coming back with her scent, with her.

The vampire baited him, unaware of what a tenuous hold he had on his beast. Unware that if he changed, he'd be unable to distinguish friend from foe, and he'd tear them all apart.

But that wouldn't save his mate. That would ruin her. And in turn ruin him. So he fought against the change, against himself, barely listening to the words fluttering around him. He forced himself to latch on to Sophie's scent, her heartbeat, her life. It was there now. It wouldn't leave.

He would make sure of that.

⁂

SOPHIE WAS BARELY able to hold on to her uterus when the wolf snatched her out of the air and slammed her against a brick wall with enough force to crack one of her ribs. Three were already broken, but to be fair, she'd cloaked her injuries from him to make sure he didn't get that tortured artist look about him whenever she had a hangnail, or a caved-in chest.

Now, out of anger, and desire, and also because she didn't have enough juice anymore, she removed the cloak.

She had been outside to say goodbye to Isla and the rest of the vamps, and to make sure that no more attackers lingered in the night. And, to be truthful with herself, she needed to leave the proximity of the book, of the premonition that had gripped her in her office.

The wolf had, of course, followed, staying silent as everyone left. And then he'd grabbed her.

She knew he sensed her injuries, but that didn't stop him from sinking his hands into her hair and laying his mouth atop of hers.

The fire of his touch was like nothing in the world. Cracked and broken ribs meant less than nothing with his tongue moving against hers, with his beast growling at the back of his throat.

She forgot all promises of death she'd hurled at him if he did this again. The only time she'd kill him now was if he stopped.

Her teeth nipped at his lips, aching to draw blood.

He moved a hand from her head downward to brutally caress her breast, causing a rush of desire to pool inside her. She cried out into his mouth. He tweaked her nipple and her knees weakened.

Then he moved lower and delved into her soaking panties. They both let out a hiss.

"Always wet for her man," he rasped.

"Her *wolf*," she corrected, mad with pleasure. She barely noticed the jerk in his body at her words, too far gone for anything but the pursuit of orgasm.

His pause was less than a second, because he found her clit and began to circle it.

"Conall," she cried out, throwing her head back. It met his palm as he took care not to let her make impact with the brick wall. He was obviously concerned about pain, but how could there be pain? Not now. Not ever.

Her climax smashed into her with the force of a thousand pickup trucks, and she cried Conall's name into the night, barely able to stay upright. She suspected the wolf was helping her with that.

She was unaware of how long it took her to come down, but she did become painfully lucid the moment her wolf stepped back, hitting her with the cold, empty air that was a slap compared to his inferno and rock-solid body.

His member strained against his jeans. His body had grown, changed with his need, and his eyes glowed.

She yearned for him to take her against the wall as much her next breath. But he'd stepped back.

She blinked once, then twice. "You... what are you doing?" she said, her words slightly slurred, as if drunk.

His jaw was stone. It took him long moments to respond, as if he physically couldn't speak. "I will not break my vow to you."

Sophie blinked again, her body still quaking from her orgasm. "You already did," she pointed out the obvious, and she wasn't even mad about it. She only wanted more. She only wanted him inside her.

He let out a pained growl, as if he could read her thoughts. He likely could sense the spike in her arousal. The connection that she usually cursed—or tried to—only excited her more in that moment.

"I did not," he gritted out. "Your power was depleted. You were hurt. Vulnerable. I knew there was no way you'd accept my help." He shrugged. "I gave it to you a different way."

Sophie gaped at him. "You think giving me an orgasm would help the fact that my power was depleted and I was hurt?" she exclaimed. It might not have done that, but it had totally helped her mood.

He nodded once. Curtly. Still holding on to control. Clutching it, more likely.

She huffed. "You're insane. And that means a lot coming from me. I'm friends with Isla, after all."

He continued to stare for the longest of moments. Sophie hated that. His brooding silences. But she wouldn't admit that she kind of loved them too. "Note your pain," he said finally.

Sophie jutted her chin up in defiance, on principle. Orders didn't go well with her. But she found herself obeying because she didn't have a choice. Her ribs, which had been burning before, were only a dull ache. Annoying, but manageable.

Then something else jumped up at her.

Power.

She had been sure she'd need days to recharge after the fight at the bar, and the little incident with seeing into the future and past at the same time back at her office.

That had been somewhat of a tight moment, as Thorne was already pissed about Isla almost dying again and the fact that not only had Sophie not been able to heal her, but she'd spewed blood everywhere when she'd tried to feed her a human who wasn't Thorne.

Note to self, being cursed by witches not only increases the chance of death, it also makes for some strict dietary requirements.

The air was tense when Sophie babbled about the end of the world and the chosen one and all that. Plus she'd let Rick, Isla, Thorne, Scott, Duncan and Conall in on what she'd found out from the book.

Obviously not the fact that she'd lost twelve hours having it imprinted in her mind. They were already freaked the fuck out.

Conall was near the point of madness, and it was all out of concern for her. She had a feeling the end of the world was nothing more than details—it was the end of her that bothered him.

She hadn't even started on the impending sense of doom that was near choking her. There was enough on her chest and on her shoulders.

Just the fate of humanity and all that.

So it was more than a little fair that she was almost running on empty when Conall had all but dragged her into the alley behind her office.

But it had returned. Not full juice, but she was able to heal her ribs with enough left over to conjure herself a cheeseburger if she so wished.

Or a thousand.

Conall gave a self-satisfied raise of his eyebrow.

She glared at him, stomping past him in a rage, only just restraining the urge to give him lupus. Or rabies.

She didn't have enough juice for that *and* a cheeseburger.

"You're seriously arrogant enough to think that giving me an orgasm will somehow charge me up like a hybrid car?" she spat, covering the fact that she was more hurt that he didn't want to actually do the nasty for, like, normal reasons.

Though she couldn't exactly ignore his desire. She knew he wanted her. But she was a female in the midst of a rage, so logic didn't factor in.

"Arrogant much?" she asked over her shoulder when she decided she was going to storm into the night and he followed behind her. "Maybe I'm a little double-a battery that doesn't need fucking charging."

He yanked her arm. "You know this was us. Me. Our connection. Do not deny it."

Again she jutted her chin up, burning his hand with enough heat to flay the skin and make him let go. "If my lawyer taught me anything, it's deny, deny, deny."

His anger blanketed Sophie's back, and then he was in front of her, blocking her path. "I did not do that just to heal you, though it was a mitigating factor. That, and watching you come is the single most magnificent thing on this planet," he growled.

Sophie's stomach dipped without permission.

"I did it so you could be unhurt while explaining to me what the fuck is going on," he roared. He stepped forward, his anger no longer checked for her, his beast rising inside him, and outside him.

Sophie did not step back, even though she felt the tiniest pinch of fear with his anger.

"And so I may tan your fucking hide for keeping things from me," he continued, voice full of promise.

Sophie's stomach dipped again.

She swallowed.

"I wasn't keeping anything from you," she said, "because it's none of your business."

"*You're* my business," he snapped. "And you getting attacked by rebels and then possessed by a fucking prophecy is *my fucking busi-*

ness. So start talking. Now." He stepped forward again. "Do not make me force you."

She smiled, calling upon the power that his fingers at her clit had replenished. "I'd like to see you try, wolf."

He didn't back down, even though her power filtered through the air in warning. The wolf was fearless. Or an idiot.

Their standoff lasted a handful of silent minutes. She knew he was comfortable in silence, preferred it even, especially when it was coupled with intense stares. Sophie was not comfortable in silence. In fact, she hated it.

Especially coupled with intense stares.

So of course, she proverbially blinked first.

"Fine," she huffed, letting her arms fall to her sides and her power recede.

Conall blinked the beast from his eyes.

He waited.

She glared at him.

"Well, it all started with my bestie, Isla."

His jaw hardened. "I *knew* she was trouble."

Sophie bristled. "Of course she is. Why do you think I'm friends with her?" Her eyes narrowed. "And you'll play nice with my vampire if you're attached to your head."

He didn't answer, and she took that as her cue to get him up to speed on the whole witchy bitchy situation.

It was safe to say he wasn't impressed once all was said and done.

Which was why Sophie had kept one important part of the prophecy to herself. One that, when she read it, caused a low chill to settle over her bones.

There will be one who takes Death's embrace like a lover's caress, and the animal within the two will roar at the moon, for its agony will blanket the earth.

Chapter Seven

Sophie had work to do.
A lot of work.
Like figure out a way to locate and kill some of the strongest witches known to the craft.
Research on how one un-mated with werewolves.
And she had to watch the second season of *Stranger Things*.
She'd told Isla that she'd contact her coven to get some more information, but she'd failed to mention that her coven wasn't exactly on the best of terms with her right then since she'd blasted in and stolen the most sacred book they had.
She didn't tell Isla because then Isla would get all distracted about the fact that they were trying to haul her back in with force, and then Isla would get distracted by trying to kill them all. As she'd been promising to do ever since Hazel insulted her hair fifty years back.
And even more so when she'd learned that they sequestered witches whose powers of premonition or something similar became powerful enough to wield as a weapon.
Isla was a protective friend, no matter how much she tried to

portray the opposite. She wouldn't hesitate to put herself in more danger to eliminate Sophie's entire coven. But she already had one lot of big bad witches after her, plus a death spell hanging over her head.

Sophie could handle this on her own.

So she called them.

"You have some gall," Nora said, her voice ice.

Sophie grinned. "I know, right?"

There was crackling silence on the other end of the phone. Sophie knew her old mentor was thirsty for revenge, to imprison Sophie, to punish her. She was archaic like that. But she was also angry that she didn't have enough power to do any of those things. Which was why Sophie hadn't gotten any magical strike-backs.

Yet.

It was only a matter of time.

She'd already cast magical burglar alarms all around her residences and offices. Plus she was on high alert for any curses directed her way. That was the *last* thing she needed.

But the plus side was they'd need her blood or to be in her immediate vicinity to curse her.

Sophie had been very careful to destroy her blood whenever it was spilled—and tried not to get it spilled if she could help it—for that particular reason. The coven was too cowardly to face off with her until they'd found more power.

"You stole our most treasured possession," Nora hissed. "That is unforgiveable. You will be punished for that."

Sophie rolled her eyes. "Okay, let's save empty threats and blood feuds for another day. We've got bigger witches to fry." Sophie's eyes caught a flash of movement at her front door.

Her wolf had broken in.

Again.

And he was bleeding. That was kind of her fault. She'd rigged a bunch of knives to blindly stab at anyone who strolled through her magical locks.

He'd dodged most of them.

She ignored his angry glare.

"You've heard of the Herodias sisters, I assume," Sophie said, focusing on the conversation with the witch who wanted to sequester her instead of the wolf who wanted to sex her.

She pretended she didn't want to sex him right back as he prowled toward her.

Nora's swift intake of breath took up the static.

"I'm taking that as a yes," Sophie said, eyeing the wolf as he didn't rip the phone from her hands as she expected. He just stood there, waiting for her to finish her phone call, bleeding all over her favorite rug. "Well, we've got somewhat of a pickle with them being involved in the revolution and the plot to enslave all of humanity," Sophie addressed Nora, her eyes drinking in the wolf. He looked hot, even with stab wounds. "So I did have kind of a good reason to steal the book." She paused. "And I also did want to get a teeny bit of revenge for you being such a raging bitch to me my entire childhood. But my motivations were *almost* entirely selfless."

More static.

Sophie let out a long sigh. "You're going to make me come out and say it, aren't you?" she asked. "Bitch," she muttered under her breath. "I need your help. I need to locate the last of the sisters. A binding spell wouldn't go astray either."

"Why in Goddess would you want to *locate* those evil creatures?" Nora exclaimed.

Sophie rolled her eyes again, then let them go over the wolf stalking around the room, staring at her.

Her thighs quivered from the stare alone.

"Uh, duh, so I can kill them and then cement my awesomeness for generations to come," she replied. "And then also stick it to you for telling me I'd never amount to anything." Another pause. "Oh, and I guess to save humanity too."

There was a cold laugh at the other end of the phone. "They cannot be defeated. Especially by you."

"You want the job?" Sophie asked. "I'd contract it out to you, you know, if you had enough power, which you don't. Doesn't that just twist your knickerbockers?"

Sophie could almost taste the angry curl in Nora's lip. "Our coven does not support fallen witches. And you will receive no knowledge from us on this matter."

Sophie's amusement turned. "Seriously?" she hissed. "You're really that concerned with your ego and your own personal feelings toward me that you'd hold back *knowledge*? From a fellow witch trying to do good?" *Well, mostly good.* "You really have abandoned everything that our kind holds sacred in your quest to get a spot on the council." Disgust saturated Sophie's tone.

Knowledge was something shared freely between all witches for centuries, no matter what. There was no room for personal grievances. Whoever made the rules had enough foresight to know a lot of women over centuries were gonna get catty. So it was made law that knowledge was the most precious thing in the craft, and as long as a sister witch was looking to serve The Four and humankind with that knowledge, it could not be denied.

It was a rule even *Sophie* didn't break.

Only bent it now and then.

"Oh, I'll be on the council," Nora sneered. "And I'll make sure the vote for you getting sequestered is the first thing that goes to pass."

On that, she hung up the phone.

"Well fuck you very much," Sophie said, throwing her phone on the table.

The wolf was in front of her in an instant, though not touching her of course. He was staying true to his word, as he had since the night of the bar fight. She hated that. And then hated herself for hating it.

She grinned at his wound, only just closing. "In case you didn't get the message, when a girl puts out a booby trap equipped with knives, that's the sign she's just not that into you."

He searched her face, which was free of makeup, and it made her uncomfortable. She almost always had her battle mask on, even when she woke up, likely leftover from the night before. The only way you can achieve a truly kickass smoky eye was to sleep in it.

I woke up like dis.

But she'd given herself one of her rare pampering, no-people days. So her hair was flat, shiny, free of product. Her face was freshly washed of the face mask she'd put on. And she was wearing an oversized men's shirt, high-waisted panties and knee-high socks.

By the look of her wolf's gaze, he liked dressed-down Sophie.

And more than liked it, if the hard-on tenting his jeans was anything to go by.

He rubbed his hand across his mouth in an inherently human movement that jarred Sophie slightly. She'd always considered him a wolf, because he was always so wild around her; there was never a moment when his beast was fully caged. But such a gesture reminded her that he wasn't just an animal.

And that was annoying.

Because now she was thinking of him as her wolf *and* her man.

Not good.

He looked as if he was going to growl at her to beg, and she feared in that state, she just might. Desire already pulsated through her blood.

"Sequestered?" he clipped instead.

That shocked her. Obviously wolves had superhuman hearing, so he'd listened to the conversation. She had no secrets—well, none a wolf could hear on a phone conversation, anyway—so she didn't really care.

So much had happened the night before that he'd somehow missed them talking about it amongst prophecies and the end of the world. She thought she'd dodged a bullet on that one.

It seemed not.

She crossed her arms.

"To isolate, shut one away, or segregate," she parroted a dictionary definition in an effort to hide her very real fear of such a thing. "Usually it's self-imposed by people who hate people, and a sister can relate to that, because people are the *worst*. But this is forced by the council that governs our kind." She swallowed. "More specifically on witches who have extraordinary magic that has the power for destruction, and the curse of foresight."

Her skin crawled with the realization that the reason the rule existed was Malena. The witch who had those qualities. The same ones Sophie had.

She shook off the undeniable connection between her and the evil bitch.

I'm not evil. Yeah, sometimes I curse people for fun, but it's mostly to have a bad hair day or to chip a tooth, and I almost always take it back. That doesn't make me evil.

Doesn't make you good either, logical Sophie chimed in.

Shut up, all the other Sophies hissed.

"You have these powers," Conall said.

"Well spotted, wolf. You should get a gold star for your powers of observation."

He stepped forward, or rather he stayed in place while his energy seemed to separate from him, pressing into her with force.

Again, that was impossible.

But that didn't mean she didn't feel the inferno of his touch on her while his hands fisted at his sides.

"They will not take you," he declared.

"Of course they won't. I'm not gonna let that happen. I'm a free-range witch," Sophie replied.

His eyes swirled. "I will not let anything happen to you."

She glared at him. "You need to stop. Stop with all of this." She waved her hand at him and stomped over to her bar to grab the whisky she'd poured in preparation for the phone call. Pamper days always included whisky. As well as every other day.

"I do not *need* protecting. I do not need a shadow in the form of a wolf." She drained her drink. "I don't need you," she hissed. "You need to realize that, and then leave me the fuck alone."

"You can lie to yourself," he growled, stepping forward.

She stepped back and hated herself for doing so. Never in her life had she retreated. Until this man.

"You can lie to those you call friends."

Another step.

That time she called on her power and stood her ground.

"But you can never lie to me," he continued, moving through the wall of pure energy she'd conjured like it was nothing more than mist.

She knew it would've ground at his very bones, that it should've crumpled him to the floor, but it did not. No, he was in front of her, clutching at her cheeks, and she was frozen in place.

"I can taste your truth in the air. Scent it in your sweet arousal every time your little body craves me." He let out a guttural growl and pushed his erection into her stomach. "See through everything you coat those eyes with to hide your heart from the world. I can do all of this because you are fated to be mine. You fight it, you battle for it, but it will not change the truth. And it will not make me stop. Nothing short of death will do that."

"I am not an animal like you," she hissed. "I am not a slave to the beast that tells me who I am bound to."

He regarded her. "Oh yes you are, *piccola soldata*. You are a slave to your beast. Just because it doesn't change you on the outside doesn't mean it doesn't exist. I can sense it. See it. And it belongs to me. And I to it."

He gave her a long and pointed look that told her he saw a lot more than even the mirror showed her.

Then he left.

Sophie had to actively catch herself from chasing after him.

Shit was *not* going well.

And they still had the baddest witches in all existence to deal with. She was more ready to deal with them than the complicated emotions she was battling with about her wolf.

Shit, why could she not stop thinking of him like that?

As *hers*?

❧

SOPHIE SAT cross-legged in the middle of the heptagram she'd drawn in rock salt. The shape itself was extremely powerful in her craft, which was the reason for the rock salt and the white candles burning on every available surface. A couple of deep purple candles also burned around them, evenly spaced. Although it was dangerous to invite the power they conducted into the room, she needed them since they helped to fuel the power of divination. Hence the heavy dose of white, and the buckets of sea salt she'd had shipped in from Greece.

She needed the purity of the objects to cast away anything attracted to Sophie's power, and to cast away the worst of Sophie's power itself, the thing inside her she had yet to learn how to control.

She failed to feel bad about her lack of action toward the power unrealized that might have the power to destroy her and everything around her. She'd been busy. She'd get around to it once she'd stopped the enslavement of humanity.

She was using the heptagram for the purpose of seeing the

future. That in itself was risky business—on the occasion that it worked. Nine times out of ten, the spell did nothing but make sure you had a sore ass from sitting too long and a lot of salt to vacuum up.

Or for someone else to vacuum up.

Sophie didn't clean.

But Sophie reasoned a lot of things had changed since the last time she'd used the spell in the sixties to see if her bob and bangs were really going to be as timeless as she'd been told by a certain member of The Kinks.

Now she'd not only manipulated time to see a glimpse of what was ahead in it, she'd fricking *traveled through it*. Granted, it was not on purpose, and Sophie had been dropped smack-dab in the middle of London in the 1900s. Not her first choice. Or her two hundredth. Did you know how bad that place smelled before they'd put in a sewer system? Isla starting that great fire on Pudding Lane was the best thing that had happened to Londoners' nostrils.

She had yet to take any jaunts through the ages since. She really hoped she'd learn how to drive the proverbial DeLorean, because she wanted to ride a dinosaur at some point. Maybe even take Isla. But knowing her vampy bestie, she'd inadvertently step on the wrong plant or kill the wrong Neanderthal and fuck up the future. So of course she'd be coming.

Sophie reasoned that since she had the ability to travel through time and spout out prophecies from millennia ago, she could get a *tiny* peek at what was in store for them, maybe even a glimpse at how future Sophie managed to figure out a banishing spell or potion.

She wasn't going to trouble herself with the fact that this probably wouldn't pan out under the whole time-travel-rules scenario. She didn't need to know the rules to break them.

She sat toward the top of her heptagram, facing the metaphorical sun and the sign for Sunday. It then went clockwise, each point representing a planet and its corresponding day of the week. Venus—Friday, Mercury—Wednesday, the Moon—Monday, Saturn—Saturday, Jupiter—Thursday and Mars—Tuesday.

She was clutching a mug filled with the dark liquid that would work as the conductor of her spell.

It wasn't blood. Yes, witches needed a sacrifice to perform rituals, but only dangerous magic required blood. This was a hefty swig of her last bottle of aged whisky that was more precious than her blood.

Technically she was meant to have a ceremonial glass goblet, but she'd smashed it one night when she'd filled it with tequila and went hunting for rogue goblins Isla accidently set loose after too many margaritas. She'd reasoned she'd need even more tequila to get them back than she'd drunk to let them out.

Instead of the centuries-old goblet, she was using a coffee mug that read 'Working Harder than an Ugly Stripper'—it was almost the same.

"Philyra, ancient witch, I call to thee," Sophie began, calling to the goddess of divination—otherwise known as her great ancestor. She had powerful blood but wasn't one to brag. "To show me the future I cannot see." Power wound around the words, even with the horrific rhyme, and the salt started to vibrate and roll on the wooden floor. "Take me through the door for which you hold the key, show me the future I cannot see."

Sophie's voice deepened as more power drained from the candles and the points of the heptagram came into her being.

The grains of salt shot into the air, keeping their perfect shape, only now in Sophie's direct eye line. Which kind of meant it was working.

The fact that she was no longer in the middle of her apartment, wondering if the red couch was really the best aesthetic choice for the energy of the room, *really* meant it was working.

She was standing barefoot on cool stone. The air was sharp enough with ice that it seemed to freeze her skin on contact. She glanced down. She was naked. Seeing the future obviously meant that you weren't allowed to wear anything from the past, even an awesome Metallica tee sweat on by James Hetfield himself.

The room she stood in was empty. It looked to be a dungeon. She was facing a wall with bloody shackles fastened to the stone. More blood was pooled on the floor underneath them, fresh, shiny enough that Sophie reasoned she could check her lipstick in it if she so wished.

She had the strongest feeling that blood belonged to someone close to her. Someone she loved. That someone was right in front of her, despite the fact that the closed shackles were empty. It made no sense, but she knew, deep inside her, that this travel to the future was only being seen with her third eye—her witch's eye. Her two human eyes were closed for now.

She suspected it may be enough to slip into madness if they were opened. That was the reason divination was practiced with such caution, because it had the very real power to send a witch off the deep end.

Sophie had been doing the backstroke in the deep end since birth. Plus she was already mad.

But she didn't want to be straitjacket mad.

And she didn't have the shoulders for it, so she didn't try to fuck with her lack of vision. She was there for a reason, so she just needed to wait and pay attention.

The stone around her was obviously old—it smelled damp, and predominantly like suffering and death. That didn't really narrow it down.

She turned, seeing nothing in the room but the manacles and a table with shiny instruments, all designed for torture, all covered in fresh blood.

Her stomach roiled at the sight of it, something telling her with even more conviction that this blood, this pain, this death, belonged to someone very close to her.

"You're not tempted?" a male voice suddenly asked, making Sophie's heartbeat pound a little harder at her rib cage.

So she wasn't alone.

The voice was smooth, accented, cruel, and not at all familiar.

"Tempted to make you eat your own dick?" a sarcastic voice shot back, not betraying an ounce of pain or fear. "Yeah, I would say it's enticing. It's one of the many options I'm tossing between before I kill you." There was a pause. "I'm still brainstorming, though, so don't get your hopes up."

Sophie knew that voice. It was that of her best friend. And so was the blood that punctured the air, the freshness of it telling her that more was being spilled.

Then the voices disappeared. The room moved slightly, but somehow stayed in the same place. Wind blew Sophie's hair into her lip gloss—she hated when that happened—even though she was pretty sure they were underground.

She guessed it was the future's way of telling her they were fast-forwarding.

As abruptly as it started, the wind stopped. The room stilled, if it had ever been moving in the first place. Sophie held her stomach, telling herself to hold on to her Cheerios.

The blood had faded now, sank into the stone so it was a dark copper stain. Though there was more of it than before. A lot more.

Sophie's stomach roiled with dread.

No. Isla was not going to die. Not again. She'd done that enough.

Sophie gritted her fists, expecting them to crackle with power. They did not. She glanced down. They weren't glowing with anything but a regular vitamin D deficiency.

She obviously didn't have powers there. Maybe since she wasn't really there.

She didn't have time to think on that because chaos swirled in the air. Dread punched Sophie in the stomach. She sensed it—death. It blanketed the room, and she was certain something was meeting its end in a matter of seconds. She couldn't see the people in the room, but she could sense their panic, their anger, their utter despair.

The manacles rattled as someone thrashed against them, the sound of the metal on the stone jarring.

"I will kill you for this," Isla promised, her voice thick with rage. And something else. Pure fear.

"No, *mon ange*," the voice purred. "You will not."

And then there was the unmistakable sound of a knife cutting through soft flesh.

"No!" Isla screamed, her voice so guttural, so full of pain, Sophie doubled over.

Blood bloomed at the stone below her. She blinked, touching her neck, bringing her fingers up to her face.

They were crimson.

Another energy engulfed the room in a sorrow so palpable that it shook the walls, the very fabric of the future.

Tears streamed down Sophie's eyes at the familiarity of it.

The howl brought her to her knees.

The howl of her wolf.

Of his utter undoing.

At her death.

Then the room disappeared, as did the blood of her death.

But not her death itself. That hung around her like a promise.

She was overcome with certainty that the vision, the knowledge of it, would not change a thing.

"You were not sent here to change this future," a voice whispered in her ear. It was sultry. Deep. Full of the ages of the earth. Of knowledge of past and future. "You were sent to witness. Tell no one of what you saw. Death cannot be cheated, pain cannot be avoided, and sorrow cannot be prevented. You know this. Use the knowledge for what you will."

Then the lips at her ears were gone.

She wanted to scream in frustration. Why did gods think that just because they were all powerful, they had to speak in riddles?

What was wrong with saying, 'Sucks that you died. Don't tell anyone, but here's the skinny on how to kill the witches'?

She didn't have time to lament on that before she was slammed back into her physical body. Her limbs screamed with the assault of having them in the same position for an undetermined amount of time. Moonlight crept into the room. It had been morning when Sophie sat down.

Her ass was numb.

And she decided that yes, the sofa was a bad choice as she pushed her aching limbs into an upward position.

"I'm thinking purple's better," she muttered to herself, intending on stepping forward out of the mess of salt around her.

But then her vision blurred. Double. Triple versions of the room.

Too many red sofas.

"Sophie!" her wolf bellowed.

There were three of him too, all sprinting toward her.

But then there was none of him because she was no longer in that time or space.

She was in the middle of something that had not yet come to pass; she knew this because the future had a cold and chaotic quality to it, as if she were standing on a lake not quite frozen yet. It was not certain whether this path would be taken or if the choices of those in the present would melt it away.

But then she was wrenched back out of that strange future that was nothing like the one she'd been hanging out in and obviously died in. She was confronted with gold fire.

"Sophie," Conall demanded, his hands at her cheeks, gripping her head.

She blinked. "Did you break in again? That's rude."

He gaped at her, his anger taking over whatever desperate concern he'd been feeling.

Something stabbed at Sophie at the reminder of his concern and pain so much greater than his concern right now.

"You are in danger," he growled as she struggled to extract herself from his arms. It wasn't successful since her limbs were jelly. "Your power, it is trying to end you." His eyes seemed to see the thing inside her that Sophie's true eye couldn't see.

But of course that was impossible.

She glared. "I'm fine."

He ran his hands over her body, as if he didn't believe her, as if she was hiding some grievous bodily wound. She let him do his check because she sensed she wouldn't be able to stop him anyway. Also, his hands on her, warm and alive, were comforting, chasing away the chilling grasp of the grave.

His palms spanned her hips, pressing into them, lifting her as he moved to stand. She tested her ability to take her own weight with his hands still gripping her, keeping her upright.

She glanced down at her purple polished toes and frowned at her feet for slacking on the job. Then she moved her eyes up to meet Conall's, every part of her desperate to drink him in while she still could.

They stayed like that, staring at each other, as if he was imprinting every part of her onto his brain too, as if he had seen her death too.

Of course he didn't.

She was about to open her mouth and say something, but he gripped the back of her head and yanked her into his iron chest, on which she somehow landed softly as both of his tree trunk arms circled her body, clutching her to him. She expected to fight, but found herself physically unable to do so. Not because his arms made that impossible—they did—but because she didn't *want* to. She needed to be wrapped in his embrace, breathe in the woodsy scent that was unique to him.

Her wolf.

He laid his lips softly on her head.

She squeezed her eyes shut and let herself sink into the moment.

He released her eventually. Her feet had regained their ability to hold the rest of her body up. Good thing too, because she couldn't be relying on the wolf to hold her up. That was dangerous. Every woman—every witch—needed to know how to stand on her on two feet; if you relied on a man, or wolf, you'd always end up meeting the floor, heart first.

She stepped backward, out of his embrace, needing the distance. She needed to because he needed it. She was going to die, there was no way around it, but that didn't bother her even half as much as the memory of his pain. His utter destruction.

She knew the goddess said that she couldn't change what she saw, but goddesses didn't know everything. Surely even they fucked up sometimes.

He frowned at her, his face tight. "There is something inside of you that you cannot control," he said, voice low and gravelly.

She quirked her brow. "Oh, hey, pot." She waved. "There's a kettle the exact shade of wolf that's in this season."

His jaw tightened. "I cannot control my beast fully, but it is not working to destroy me. It is *part* of me."

She jutted her chin up at the disgust in his tone, toward the very thing that made her... her. Yes there were dangerous parts of it that may eviscerate everything she knew about herself, but nobody was perfect. She bet his wolf ruined countless pairs of jeans.

"As my magic is a part of me."

Again with that intense perusal. He stepped forward so he could grasp her again, as if he was scared she might just float away.

That made two of them.

"Yes, you were born to be a powerful witch. That is apparent in everything about you. But this danger I sense inside of you does not come from birth, it comes from death. And it brings it." His hands dug into her forearms. "And I will do everything I can to make sure that doesn't happen. Even if it makes you hate me." Again with the intense look. "I won't lose you."

She wrenched herself from his grasp, hating that his strength would always be used against her. Then again, her power could always be used against him—the one he was insinuating he was going to destroy, *no freaking way*—so she did just that, and froze him in place.

"You can't lose something you've never had, wolf," she said, the lie bitter on her tongue. Because he did have her. Completely and utterly. But it was important not to admit that to him. More important not to admit that to herself.

She grinned in satisfaction as only his eyes moved. She could see the thrashing of his aura as the beast inside of him rebelled at being in such a state. She imagined he might be very pissed off depending on how long she kept him like that.

I can have some fun with this.

"I'm off to make some battle plans at the home of the vampire king tonight," she told the Conall statue before sauntering over to her mirror, making sure she swayed her hips. His gaze was like a brand.

"And obviously I can't wear this to meet a king and plan to overthrow a rebellion," she said, glancing at her ripped tee in the mirror. She squinted over her shoulder at the wolf, a nudge against her spell telling her that he was fighting tooth, nail, and tail to get out of it.

Obviously he couldn't.

But Hades did love a trier.

She made sure he could see the front of her in the reflection of the mirror before she yanked the tee over her head and sent it fluttering to the floor.

Another nudge against her spell as she stood in her bra—purple lace so sheer, her hardened nipples almost punctured the delicate fabric—and jeans.

She trailed her hand down the middle of her chest, between the ridges of her breast bone, her breaths becoming shallower at the power she had over Conall.

And not just the spell rendering him immobile. No, it seemed she didn't need a spell to make his eyes devour her with a reverence akin to a man meeting his god.

It unnerved and *excited* her.

She undid the front clasp, dropping her bra to the ground, and the cold air assaulted her hard nipples.

That time there was no nudge against her spell—there was an almighty slam. She'd been prepared, so she held onto it.

Barely.

She hooked her thumbs into her jeans, bending slowly to yank them to her ankles, pushing her hips upward and thanking Goddess for all those squats she did that one time ten years before.

When she straightened and kicked her jeans away, her eyes met Conall's molten gold ones.

Was it Conall or the beast? Was there a difference?

She stood only in her panties, which were drenched from the electricity in the air, from the pure and utter sensual act of stripping for her wolf while he could do nothing but watch.

He was thrashing against her spell now, and she was having trouble controlling it. It said nothing about her power, and everything about his desperation to go to her. She ached for him so bad that she almost released her grip on the spell, let him have his way, finally sate that hunger both of them had been battling against.

But no.

That meant that pesky ownership agreement.

That meant *begging*.

So instead, she called up more power and tightened her grip on the spell. Her hands trailed the top of her panties as she continued to gaze at her wolf through hooded lashes.

Shit, there she was thinking of him as her wolf again.

"I think I might have to change these too, no?" she asked innocently, blinking at the wild eyes.

"Release me, *luna mia*," he commanded. His words were thick and guttural. Barely human, as the human inside him was bound with her magic.

Her hand froze at the top of her panties, which had just become even wetter at his desperate tone. He should not have been able to speak. She'd had some of the strongest demons on earth in the grip of that spell and they hadn't even been able to blink as Isla or Sophie herself cut their heads off. Desire to *live* wasn't even strong enough to fight Sophie's spell.

But Conall's desire for her was.

She recovered quickly, licking her lips and gazing at him. "I think not, *piccolo lupo*," she replied. Then, before her strength failed her, she yanked her panties down her legs, biting her lip as she brushed her sensitive clit.

The air thickened to the point that it almost became unbreathable.

Sophie sucked in the thick energy of her wolf's desire. Then she turned, giving his eyes a feast.

"Come. To. Me," he gritted out.

She almost did. His entire body was covered in a thin sheen of sweat, but instead of being grossed out by it, the glistening muscles turned her on even more. Everything was taut, ready to spring, battling against the unseen cage. His eyes were molten gold, heat seeping out of them and directly into her. Everything inside her told her it was right to go to him.

But she never did what was right.

Why start now?

"Sorry, wolf, I've got an appointment to keep."

And she turned on her heel and walked in the opposite direction toward her small closet.

His growls echoed with every step, a physical slap against her aching need.

But she ignored it.

She had to.

She was rather attached to surviving, and she wouldn't do so if she surrendered to the wolf.

As she slipped into her clothes in the next room, her hold over the spell grew more and more tenuous, which should have been impossible. Why was this wolf continuing to show her that there were no rules when it came to them? She hated rules on principle, but her magic was her constant. Yes, it was getting pretty scary and uncontrollable. But not defeatable.

Even the most powerful witches she'd encountered so far weren't a match for her. He held no magic, yet he challenged hers.

He was still a statue—albeit an angry one—when she sauntered into the room a handful of minutes later, having regained her composure and dressed in a kickass outfit.

His eyes flared at what she was wearing.

"You are not leaving in that," he ground out, focusing on her leather hot pants that laced at the front and showed a generous amount of butt cheek. Her boots went almost to the tops of her thighs—think a goth version of X-Tina's "Dirty"—so Sophie reasoned it evened out.

She snatched her purse, grinning at him. "Pesky wolf, you keep thinking you've got say over... well anything," she tutted. "It doesn't work that way with this witch. The sooner you realize that and move on, the better."

She turned on her heel and strutted from the room. It was only when she reached the front door that he spoke once more, breaking her spell again.

"You know there is no moving on from this, *luna mia*."

She froze, her hand on the doorknob.

She itched to stay and argue, scream that he was wrong. But she didn't have the energy for that kind of lie, and she needed her energy. Who knew what she would encounter at the king's compound.

So instead of doing something she wanted to do, like cross the room and kiss him and then surrender, she walked out, in search of a battle that was a lot less dangerous than whatever was between her and Conall—like the end of life as she knew it.

꽃

ONE WEEK LATER

"You have to tell me where she is," an angry male voice demanded.

Not the angry male voice she'd wanted.

There were just too many around these days.

She glanced up from her computer where she was gaining intel the new-fashioned way. Who knew, maybe there was a Tumblr page dedicated to Malena.

"I'm getting rather sick of men telling me what they think I have to do," she replied to Thorne, who was rippling with panic and fury and despair. She glanced at him and felt a little bout of pity for the poor sod. He was a mess.

Okay, he wasn't a mess. He was hot as shit with his leather jacket, jacked muscles, carved cheekbones and intoxicating eyes.

But his aura was in somewhat of a frenzy. It was bad.

Then she remembered that he'd lied to Isla about being brothers with the king of the vampire race—who just so happened to be trying to make Isla his queen—and about everything he was. And he was the reason Isla had gone MIA for the past week, because she couldn't handle the heartbreak that came with betrayal.

Then she didn't feel so sorry for him.

"I'm gonna start giving overzealous males some boobs and a vagina soon, just so they know what it feels like when people think they can order women around just because they possess them," she said mildly.

Thorne ran his hand through his hair. "She is in danger, Sophie," he clipped. "She's fucking cursed and running off half-cocked."

"Half-cocked is the way Isla works best." She smiled, despite being slightly worried about the vamp running around the city solo while witches had a curse on her. "You should be happy I'm not making *you* work that way after what you did to her." Venom and sincerity saturated her tone. No one fucked with her friend and got away with it. Not with their whole penis, at least.

He crossed his arms, meeting her eyes. "I didn't mean to hurt her."

Sophie rolled her eyes. "Can you be any more cliché? That's what every fucking guy says after he hurts the woman he 'loves.' Granted, the whole 'deceiving her into thinking you're a mortal slayer when you're really the immortal and kind-of-human offspring from a vampire king and queen' thing isn't exactly the same as banging the secretary." She glared at him for a second. "But betrayal is betrayal, no matter how it's packaged."

He gritted his teeth. "I didn't exactly expect to fucking fall in love with her!" he roared. "And then when it became apparent that I could only ever have eternity with her, how did you think I could broach the subject of truth? I knew she'd act like this, that I might fuckin' lose her. I'm not losing her." It wasn't so much a promise to Sophie as a declaration to the gods.

"You don't have to convince me, dude," she said, holding her hand up. "Actually, you totally do. But first you have to get your shit together, stop hitting up my place of work, and figure out that Isla will come to you when she's ready."

"When do you think that will be?"

She grinned. "About a century, give or take a decade," she said honestly.

His eyes flashed with anger. Or maybe despair.

Sophie leaned forward. "I know Isla might act like she's bulletproof—and that's because she is. With actual bullets. With things like what you've done to her?" Sophie shook her head. "Not so much. Isla is the strongest immortal I've ever met, apart from me, of course. And it's the strongest ones who are most vulnerable. Who break the hardest when someone they trust betrays them." Sophie gave him a long and pointed look. "You better pick up the pieces and repair her as good as new, Buffy, or else you'll be ash and there won't be pieces of you for anyone to pick up."

That was another promise.

He nodded once, curtly, as if the motion pained him.

Sophie smiled. "Great, now I've got work to do." She moved her attention back to her computer.

"You're not gonna tell me where she is?" he all but shouted.

"Of course I'm not," she replied, still focused on the screen. "I'm still on her good side, and it's chicks before dicks. All day long. I'd advise you to leave while you're still intact."

He stayed for a long moment, desperation dripping off him. "I will find her," he vowed.

"Or you'll die trying," she muttered as he left.

That was the thing with these males. Death was the only thing that would stop them.

Which meant both she and Isla were fucked.

Chapter Eight

Since banishing Thorne to go rip apart the city looking for Isla, Sophie had met the vampire herself for coffee. She had not looked good. Like at all. In addition to the previously self-professed invincible badass suffering her first heartbreak in five centuries, she was also battling a serious case of the blunchies—like munchies, but with blood.

The nasty curse cast by those evil bitches meant the only blood Isla could drink was Thorne's, and after they found out it didn't actually kill her like it technically should have, all was well. It was all *Twilight* and romantic, from what Sophie gleaned.

But then Thorne had gone and fucked up, and Isla didn't want to be near him so bad that she was literally starving herself so she didn't have to see him.

It was a clusterfuck of emotions, ones Isla was not equipped to deal with. So she did what any heartbroken girl would do: went on a killing spree.

When Sophie had helped as much as she could've, she'd feigned off joining in—highly unusual—with a lie about the coven meeting.

Isla still didn't know that Sophie and the coven were technically on the outs. And she did not need to know right now. Instead, Sophie needed to get as much research in as possible about the witches, since she was still stumped on how to beat them.

She knew every inch of the damn book backward and forward, but there was no step-by-step banishing spell.

Of course, that would be far too easy.

She also had to actively not think about the wolf, who had been absent from her life for nigh on a week now. Something she technically should've been glad for.

She was horrified to find out she was not glad.

She was horrified to find out that she yearned for him, ached for him with a pain that was barely bearable. Which didn't make a lick of sense because she wasn't the one experiencing the stupid and cruel mating phenomenon.

But she yearned all the same.

And dreamed of him every single night.

Something cold curled in her stomach as to the reason for his absence. Obviously he could've just given up on Sophie, thinking she was a lost cause, and decided to get on with his life.

But Sophie's truest of hearts knew that was not the case. Something more sinister was going down.

※

ONE WEEK LATER

A lot happened in a week when you were Isla's best buddy.

Or when you were Sophie.

Since Sophie was both, a lot went down.

Isla went missing.

Twice.

After having coffee with Sophie and giving her intel about the location of someone connected to the rebellion, she dropped off the face of the earth for three days.

That was when she'd faced off against the father of all vampires.

Like, the *original* one.

Then, after a brief sarcastic phone call to stop an erratic Sophie from well and truly losing her ever-loving shit, she'd hopped on a plane to the cave where the remaining Herodias sister was imprisoned to fight her alone.

Sophie had done some quick computer hacking and a tiny bit of scrying to find out Isla was in Eastern Europe, so naturally she hopped on a private jet to back her sister up.

Naturally a wild Thorne and a reserved but still rather worried King Rick came with her.

"This is all because she's too pissed at you to ask for help," Sophie had hissed at Thorne while they weaved through the hills of Albania, heading toward the cave Sophie had found by scrying for Isla.

"Isla never asks for help. She's far too narcissistic for that. Even without her anger at Thorne, she likely would've done this anyway," Rick put in. His cultured voice was tight with worry.

At least he'd spoken. Thorne hadn't said a word since getting on the plane, nor during the two-hour ride it took to get to the place Sophie sensed was near.

The evil spreading over the landscape caked it like tar, but only for the eyes of the witch. She shivered, dread creeping up her spine. She had found no banishing spell, so she was just going to have to wing it.

She did it with her eyeliner, why not undefeatable witches who would end the world if she failed?

Sophie glared at the monarch, her eyes glowing with power she was calling up in preparation. For either a battle at Isla's side, or at the sight of her corpse. If it was the latter, both of these males were dust.

But as it happened, Isla had defeated the witch and was undead enough to boast about it. In other words, she was fine... ish.

Sophie still sensed the death magic, only stronger now since Malena was the last remaining witch and she sensed that her sisters had died.

And she was *pissed*.

Witches were most dangerous when pissed. Just ask the hairdresser who'd fucked up Sophie's bangs.

They brought a human stowaway back from the cave, apparently tortured by the witches. Sophie had sensed immediately that she wasn't *just* human, but she hadn't sensed outright malice, so she'd stayed as mute as the human. It wasn't her story to tell.

So all happy ever after.

Kind of.

Okay, not at fucking *all*.

Especially since she still hadn't found the wolf. More and more she seemed to sense he was in danger. In pain. Her dreams were telling her so. And a witch had to listen to her dreams—they were her third eye's most powerful communication tool.

So she listened. Mostly because it had become hard to breathe without knowing the wolf was alive.

Her wolf.

Isla thought she was searching for some ingredient for the binding potion for their upcoming mission to Russia. Kill Isla's family, capture the all-evil witch, your normal weekend jaunt.

But instead she was wolf hunting.

Her knife trailed along the wood of her floors as she carved out a line. "The sky is not above me, for I am the sky," she said, her voice floating with the power of the single stroke of the athame. Red seeped into the wood from the knife dripping with her blood.

That time, blood was required. And Sophie spilled it without question. It was for her wolf.

She made another line, meeting the first at the top and moving diagonally down so she made two thirds of a triangle. "The earth is not below me, for I have emerged from it, and it clings to my skin," she continued, the low burn of magic humming through her. She drew a diagonal line back upward, to the left side that time.

"The fire is within me, and it does not burn me for I use it to burn my enemies." She drew a horizontal line. "Water turns to blood and blood to water as I use the elixir of my enemies to paint my soul," she chanted, power pulsating the walls of her apartment.

She drew the last of the lines to complete her pentagram, and a sharp jolt of energy ran up the knife and into her arm, like the kickback of a shotgun. She grinned at the glowing star, pulsing purple. "And my spirit, well, that's kickass as all hell."

Images hit her brain with enough force to make her bite her tongue painfully. Blood ran down her chin and she clenched her fists laying atop her knees. She forced herself to hold the image of Conall in her mind, as other beings drawn to her power tried to claw at her skull for help.

She had cast for trapped beings, in pain, or imprisoned, and on this earth, that was most of the population, so it was safe to say her head was louder than a Nine Inch Nails concert.

Her teeth mashed together as she waded through a planet full of suffering, casting beings aside with a brutality that was required.

She couldn't save everyone.

Not even most of them.

But she would save the wolf.

Her wolf.

꽃

SOPHIE PRESSED against the exhaustion in her bones as she crunched through the woods of Sterling Forest, right in the middle of the Ramapo Mountains.

The moon dimly peeked through the dense shrubbery.

The *full* moon.

This should be interesting.

Contrary to popular belief, the full moon did not *make* the werewolves turn. In the beginning, they might've been chained to the lunar cycle. But wolves were a species, even if they were created by wrathful gods—hey, you could say the same about humans, depending which way you decided to take the creation story—which meant they evolved. To survive, to scramble their way up the food chain, they fought against the moon's pull until it no longer forced them to change.

Sophie had only just recently learned that. Right about the time a certain wolf came into her life. Of course, she'd learned about wolves in witch classes, but she'd hated every single moment of those classes, so she rebelled against retaining anything in her memory.

The moon did make wolves stronger when it was full, though. Which was both a good and a bad thing. She knew Conall was weakened, and in pain—the mere thought made her palms crackle with the need to punish someone, end someone—and the moon would give him a burst of power.

But she also sensed that those responsible for his pain might be of the wolf persuasion too, making them stronger.

Not that she was overly worried.

Because she had something in common with the wolves. Not excess body hair—she was lasered from the neck down, thank you, human technology—but the fact that *she* gained power from the moon.

Witches either derived it from the day or night, sun or moon. Two castes. Not dark and light, but more like a representative of the kind of powers Nature blessed a witch with, magicks that related to both of the life-giving planets, and each witch was more powerful either on the rising or the setting of the sun.

It just so happened that Sophie was a moon baby too.

So despite having nearly expelled all her juice while travelling to Albania and healing the human and all that jazz, Sophie was getting a pick-me-up from the moon that her wolf howled to.

A branch whipped forward unexpectedly and smacked Sophie right in the face. She glared at it and then promptly cast a spell to make the whole branch, and the tree attached to it, wither and die.

"I fucking *hate* nature," she hissed, stomping through the woods. Not very witchy of her, considering Mother Nature was the being Sophie had to thank for her powers, but whatever. Sophie had always been the bad witch, and she had to own her title.

And she *liked* nature.

Coffee came from beans. That was nature.

Vodka came from potatoes—nature.

And she lived for Ozzy. No way he came from anything but the magical nature.

Power hit her as she approached a clearing in the dense brush. She cast a quick spell to enhance her hearing. She'd already cloaked her scent before she left, mindful of the fact that werewolves could smell from great distances and it would totally fuck up her entrance if they scented her before they saw her.

"You are going to tell us, Conall," a voice rasped. There was a low buzz and a grunt.

Sophie stiffened and her palms glowed, leaves withering all around her. They were using a fucking *cattle prod* on her wolf? They were so fucking dead.

She should've stayed and listened for longer, gained more intel, had surer footing to attack on, but her fury didn't let her. Plus her footing was already fucked since she was wearing five-inch Jimmy Choos for this little nature walk.

She let go of her cloaking spell the same second she appeared in the clearing, Conall's eyes tattooed her the moment she did so, his growl echoing through the woods. Though it was animal, it was coming from his human form. His fucking battered human form.

Sophie froze for a long moment as she ran her eyes over him.

One of his eyes was swollen shut, which meant it was either a recent wound or he was too weakened to regenerate as he should. He was in a cage that thrummed with magic. It was spelled not only to stop him escaping, but to stop him changing, and stop him fucking *healing*.

It also had Nora's magical imprint all over it.

Bitch wants war, then.

He was shirtless, his muscled torso spattered with bruises and puncture wounds. Blood soaked his left arm, which hung limply as if it had been ripped from its socket.

His aura was ripped, shredded, and bleeding.

He shouldn't have been standing, let alone pounding at the bars as he started to do the second he'd seen Sophie. Elation, anger, desperation, and violence ripped through his fractured aura.

Sophie tore her eyes away from him with effort to focus on the three men in the middle of the clearing. There was not much there but a small fire, a cooler with a couple of half-drunk beer bottles atop it. And a variety of weapons.

The air buzzed with the power Sophie called up.

"Hey, boys. Little camping trip with a side of torture, is it?" she asked, sauntering forward. Insects crawled from holes in the ground, worms wiggling upward from in front of and behind her. Spiders scattered amongst the trees, advancing with a fury fueled by Sophie.

Two snakes slithered past her ankles, caressing them as she walked, hissing as they approached the suddenly pale-looking wolves. She muttered a command and the serpents both advanced on the man holding the cattle prod. He dropped it immediately to try and kick at the snakes, growling at them.

One went flying through the air as he swatted it away, the other latched onto his neck.

Sophie smiled at the other two slightly paler wolves, gaping at the creatures of the night around her.

No butterflies or ladybirds for this witch.

She grinned. "Harry Potter wasn't the only magical badass who spoke parseltongue," she said with a bite to her voice, a rumble that was familiar to the one who'd attached herself to her voice that day with Rick in the clearing. The day the power almost consumed her.

But nothing would be consuming Sophie that night. She held ironclad control over the power that had threatened to destroy her before. The moon seeped its strength into her, the natural pull giving her focus that complemented her fury perfectly.

The muscled wolves who'd originally been shocked and fearful of Sophie became less so as she strutted closer and revealed herself to be a petite, tattooed woman wearing leather hot pants and a ripped Yeezy tee shirt.

Their mistake.

As was the leer at her exposed pins.

"I will kill you for looking at my mate like that," Conall snarled from his position trying to rip at the bars.

The bald and muscled werewolf who reeked of beer and cruelty grinned. "You're mated with a *witch?*" he spat, his eyes centered on her tits. "Well I'm going to have some fun with her." He glanced to his slightly shorter and less-muscled companion, the cattle prod one still trying to wrench the snake from his neck. "We'll both take her." He glanced back to Sophie. "Don't worry, we won't hurt you—at the beginning, anyway. Wouldn't want to spoil our fun later." His words were full of male arrogance that came from a terrible upbringing, lack of brain cells, and the belief that muscles and a cock meant strength and superiority.

Sophie was so happy she was going to be the one to give him a much-needed education.

She put her hand on her hip, licking her lips and gazing at the trio through her lashes.

"People, more specifically immortal alpha males, seem to keep underestimating me," she said conversationally as the men ripped free of their human form and exploded into snarling werewolves three times their size. They advanced on her slowly. The third one had rid himself of the snake and was now sporting an angry and swollen-looking bite that had streaks of red running upward from his chin. It might kill him, the venom, but he was immortal, so it'd likely just piss him off. Sophie was not perturbed.

Conall obviously was, if the roars from inside the bars were anything to go by.

Sophie ignored him and focused on the werewolves in front of her. "I'm especially underestimated if these immortals can turn into big and scary werewolves who think they can scare little damsels like me."

Just as the wolves prepared to strike, she cast out a wave of power, knocking all three of them back at least the length of a football field. Each hit a tree—felled a tree, actually—and crumpled amongst the trunks, morphing into their human selves and not moving.

She suspected they might be napping for a hot minute.

She hadn't actually killed any of them as she itched to. It wasn't the time to go around killing immortals willy-nilly.

Not now at least.

She might come back for them later.

"Now you see I'm not a damsel. I'm actually a wolf, bigger and badder and better than any of you," she yelled at the unconscious men, for dramatic effect more than anything else.

"Sophie!" Conall roared from the bars, his skin pulsating with his need to change, to get to her.

She glanced at him. "I'm coming! Can you not let a girl have her moment?" she huffed, stomping over the leaves to get to the cage. She clung to her façade as she came closer to see exactly what those assholes had done to him.

"Okay, I'm totally changing my mind. I'm going to kill them

all," she hissed, her voice shaky. It didn't matter that she was seriously tapped out. It just meant she had to tap into something she'd been avoiding because she was scared she couldn't handle it. Scared it might destroy her.

Seeing Conall—her wolf—covered in cuts, bruises, and blood, his cheekbones gaunt and hollow from obvious lack of food, that tortured look in his golden eyes, she welcomed destruction if it meant she could get revenge.

"No," he commanded, voice so strong and sure it gave Sophie pause.

She locked eyes with Conall.

"You are not to kill them," he said. His eyes bored into her, as if he could see what she would need to do to spill death blood that night. "Unlock me, and let me feel you so I know this is not a dream. Let me fucking taste you," he snarled, his eyes wild.

A slave to his command, Sophie did just that, muttering a spell that yanked away the enchantments keeping Conall in. She was about to do the same with the rudimentary lock, but Conall ripped it off its hinges and sent it flying toward the spot where she'd tossed the men.

It fell short.

She grinned. "I can throw farther than you," she teased.

But then she wasn't grinning or teasing because her wolf pounced on her, his hands tangling in her hair, yanking her mouth to his, and absolutely ruining her with his kiss. It was like the first breath of oxygen after suffocating to death. Or the taste of water after perishing from thirst.

It was everything. The ache that Sophie had been carrying didn't diminish, though. It only increased with his nearness, her utter need for him unyielding and urgent.

"Conall," she rasped, pulling her lips back and meeting the eyes of a wolf—her wolf. She didn't flinch away, merely clutched him tighter. "I need you."

He growled, his body flexing with his need to change. She understood it then. However long he'd been trapped in there, he'd been unable to unleash his beast. She knew a wolf needed to change on a regular basis, that being deprived of such a thing was some of the worst torture imaginable.

And he was fighting that need, that intrinsic, basic need that was etched in his DNA.

Her heart slammed in her chest, her power pulsating in her fingertips, the need to kill leaving her as her need for the wolf eclipsed everything else.

"Sophie," he gritted out, his voice barely human.

She lifted her hand to stroke his cheek in a tenderness she didn't know she was capable of. She used the skin-to-skin contact to run the last of her magic through him, to knit his bones together, seal his cuts, erase his bruises. It took everything she had, even with the full moon, because she was also fighting the power she'd called up to fight with the werewolves.

Not that she cared. She would've given Conall everything.

Though he was almost beyond human comprehension, all his effort going to stopping the change. He blinked at her in amazement, then anger.

"You are not strong enough to heal me and protect yourself," he growled.

She grinned. "Well, that's what I've got a big bad wolf for." She stopped grinning. "For now, at least. This is a onetime thing, since I feel bad about not coming to your rescue sooner."

He narrowed his eyes at her, not saying anything, but she knew he wasn't at all hot on the idea of her riding in and saving the day.

"Conall," she prompted, pushing his chin up to face the moon. "I think I was promised a big bad wolf."

His eyes swirled from gold to silver, enchanted by the moon, transfixed by it. Her fingers slipped from his chin as he grew larger, his bones cracking to make room for the new ones hidden by whatever magic it was that made a man turn into a wolf.

With effort that amazed Sophie, Conall wrenched his gaze from the moon to stare at her, to stop mid-change.

"You're mine," he gritted out, his voice guttural.

She blinked at him.

He glared back in expectation, waiting despite every muscle quaking with exertion. The very moon waiting so it could take its control back.

Then Sophie realized it.

He'd stopped in the middle of one of the most strenuous and uncontrollable changes in the supernatural world to make her admit that she was his. Fuck, he took alpha male to a new level. She had a vague urge to snap Isla a pic and say, 'My boyfriend's more hardcore than yours.'

But then she would have to stop looking at the wolf.

Her wolf.

"I'm not yours," she said, taunting the beast who could literally rip her throat out. It was known to happen, even with friends and wives. When changed, things simplified for the wolves; they could still understand human words, but they could only take basic meanings from them, unable to distinguish complicated undertones.

In other words, Sophie was playing with fire. She could taste the danger in the air, so much starker than it had been with the three wolves who'd wanted to rape and kill her.

"I'm not yours," she repeated. "But you're mine."

The danger passed like a plastic bag floating away in the wind.

Conall let out a growl and then faced the moon, happy enough with Sophie's subversion on the classic alpha male declaration to let the lunar god take control.

Sophie watched, unable to look away as Conall morphed, changed, grew.

She'd never thought he'd be more magnificent—not that she had really admitted to herself that's what she thought he was until now—than what he was in his human form, everything ruggedly beautiful.

But she was wrong.

The wolf he let out of the cage of his skin was more than merely beautiful. The silken fur covering the beautiful beast was the shimmering gold of his eyes, like it had been melted down from the crowns of the most powerful of monarchs. It shined against the silver of the moon, reflecting off it.

He was larger than the wolves she'd dispatched earlier. Much larger. He towered over her, hazel-flecked eyes focused so intently on her that she could see the reflection of herself in his irises. His gaze betrayed everything that Conall—human Conall—always did; nothing was lost in his transformation. It wasn't unnatural or jarring, though. This was Conall. A beautifully dangerous and deadly part of him.

She stepped forward, lifting her hand so she could sink it into his golden fur. She shivered coming into contact with him, the warmth running through his entire form shooting into her very bones, giving her a burst of pure energy that was as natural as she had ever experienced. As pure.

It chased away the chill that calling up her grave power had given her. Chased away all that dread she'd been carrying around for months. The death that stalked her. That was attached to her very soul. Chased away everything until there was just that moment. There was just the comforting glow of the moon, the intoxicating stare of her wolf.

Just her and Conall and the woods surrounding them.

It was the most natural thing in the world for her to fist his coat while he kneeled so she could climb onto his back.

If someone had told her a handful of months ago that she'd be *riding* the werewolf who she was vaguely obsessed with, Sophie would've laughed in their face and then kicked them in the shins. Maybe cursed them with a never-ending hangnail if she was feeling sassy.

But there she was, feeling like everything in her life had built her up to that moment. Like it was a fault in fate, to put a damaged and death-stained witch with a tortured and dangerous werewolf.

Under the lingering and watchful gaze of the moon, they tore into the night.

Chapter Nine

Sophie's booted heels landed with a crunch on the gravel, the ground feeling foreign and wrong to her when she'd been flying for so long.

That's what it had been like. Hurtling through the night, above the ground, watching as the world flashed by in a blur. Utter freedom.

Witches didn't fly, whatever popular culture said. Broomsticks were literally utilized for sweeping kitchens—and in Sophie's case, snapping in half and used to impale an annoying demon.

It was addictive, that feeling. Like she'd just taken a hit of heroin—not that she'd ever done it, but she imagined this was like a drug. Total euphoria, a singing of the blood, a haze over the eyes, a rapid yet comforting heartbeat. And then it was being yanked away as the wolf in front of her shrank, sank back into the man who replaced him.

"We *have* to do that again," she breathed, eyes lazily taking in Conall's beautifully muscled and scarred body. It was healthy, fuller, more vibrant than it had ever been, like someone had come in and oiled him up to prepare for a *GQ* shoot.

Her eyes moved lower, past his delightful V pointing to the most exciting spot on a male, and then she paused, snapping her eyes back up to his. "How is it that your clothes aren't, like, ripped to shreds?" she demanded, looking at the stained and ripped jeans he'd been wearing before. "That's just totally weird."

He smirked. *Smirked!*

Well, not exactly. The corner of his mouth turned up the slightest amount. It could've been a trick of the light, but Sophie was choosing to classify that as a smirk.

He stepped forward so his hands bit into her hips and pushed her backward so the cold metal of her Jeep pressed into her back. "The woman who commanded serpents and insects is telling *me* what's weird?"

Sophie grinned at him. He was making a little joke. Who was this man? "You're in good spirits for a wolf who's literally been locked in a cage and tortured for... how long did they have you in there for?"

"Eight days, four hours, forty-eight minutes," he replied, voice rough but not full of that pain she'd expect from someone recounting their time in brutal captivity.

Anger yanked itself up Sophie's throat, burning away the elation of the moments before. "Eight days?" she repeated. She struggled against his grip. "Let me go. I'm going to find those wolves and rip their limbs apart, watch them grow them again, and then repeat the process for eight fucking *years*." She wasn't exaggerating—that's exactly what she intended on doing.

Conall stopped her.

She glared up at him. "Let me go," she demanded.

"Never," he growled.

Sophie ignored the fact that she knew he wasn't talking about that precise moment. She also ignored the fact that it filled her with the witchy equivalent of warm fuzzies.

"They tortured you, and you counted the time. Down to the minute," she clipped. "They need to pay."

He held her chin between his thumb and forefinger with a gentleness she wouldn't have thought possible from the man she'd known before. But then she'd seen it in the beast she'd met that night.

Novel, the wild beast was gentler than the man who held it prisoner.

"No, I counted the exact time I was away from my mate." His eyes burned into her, as if they were searching for any scars added to her psyche in the time they'd been apart. "Away from her when she was hunting a death that already stalked her."

She blinked at his perception. Did he know? No, he couldn't know the truth. No one knew that. Not even Isla.

He was just exaggerating, as intense alpha males tended to do. She'd once heard Thorne say, "I'm holding the future in my arms this very second. My sarcastic, infuriating, and beautiful future."

Even a *chick* wouldn't say that.

Well, not any of the chicks she hung around with. Granted, the only chicks she hung around with were Isla. And Scott.

"I've been fine. It's been boring really," Sophie lied.

He quirked his brow, calling her bluff immediately.

"Okay, so there might've been a small jaunt to Albania to kill the second of the witch sisters, but that was a little anticlimactic because Isla had already killed her without me," Sophie huffed. "Such a shitty friend move. And then there was the whole 'Thorne is actually Rick's brother but not a vampire because of some fucked-up Catch-22 that one god or another tacked onto the creations of vampires,'" she babbled. "It was a big *thing*. Honestly, even the writers of *Days of Our Lives* couldn't make this shit up. And I think Isla is still a bit pissed at Thorne, but I'm sure they'll work it out considering she needs his blood to survive and she's pretty attached to surviving. And also an age-old prophecy said they're destined to be together, so there's that." She locked eyes with golden ones. "Other than that, it's been downright dull." She furrowed her brow. "I feel like the talking stick needs to be passed to you so you can explain to me how and why the fuck you got kidnapped." Her voice held an edge to it she couldn't control.

She was punishing herself for flitting around the globe, checking out caves holding some of the worst evil known to man and beast, being mad at Conall for disappearing, then mad at herself for being mad about him disappearing, and this whole time he'd been locked up. In the fucking *woods*.

"No," he growled, bringing her closer.

She gasped as his hardness pressed into her and a hunger that she'd shoved aside in place of concern came back with a vengeance.

His hands moved to her neck. "None of that now." He trailed his thumb over her bottom lip, rubbing it until she opened it to him with a moan. "You said something before, that you needed me."

Sophie's stomach dipped with the memory, with the need that still burned more intense than her need for oxygen. "I do," she rasped.

"Are you going to beg?" he asked, running his hand down the side of her neck, trailing her collarbone and slipping into her tee so he could cup her breasts overtop of her bra.

"Never," she hissed, but her body was already yielding to him. It was a matter of moments before her mind did too.

His eyes glowed in the moonlight. Though human now, the wolf still held him in her grasp. Sophie too.

"You will," he declared, then leaned forward, claiming her mouth brutally and tenderly at the same time as his thumb tweaked her nipple.

Sophie's knees shuddered as she kissed him back with ferocity.

At some point she'd hooked her leg around his hips, yanking

him to her. But obviously not happy with the height distance, Conall lifted her with a grunt, laying her on the hood of her car so he could slam his denim-clad erection against her leather-clad core.

She cried into his mouth, her body so sensitive, so wanting, that the mere impact, even with clothes separating them, threatened to make her come.

He detached his lips from hers for the smallest of moments. Then they were back to ravaging her mouth, but somehow both her tee and bra were gone. Both his hands kneaded at her breasts before he laid his palm on her chest to push her back onto the hood of the car.

The cold metal contrasted with the inferno at her front. His form was cut from the midnight air behind him, cast in the moonlight glow above him. Like some kind of god.

"Beg," he demanded, his voice a whip.

"No," she whispered, the word lost in the night's breeze.

He let out a sound in his throat and wrapped his lips around her nipple. She tangled her hands in his hair, feeling the same softness she had when she'd sank her fingertips into the wolf's fur before.

Her entire body was on fire with her need for him, with the need for release. His tongue and teeth moved against her nipple, right to the point of climax, and then he stopped, the night air replacing his mouth.

She cried out in frustration, and he moved his head downward, trailing kisses down her navel.

"Yes," she hissed as he ripped at the fastenings of her shorts. He lifted her up in one swift move so her shoulders were pressed into the hood of the car and her butt was in the air, her panties and shorts coming off in a flash.

She was wearing only her heels and the gaze from her wolf. His eyes were glued to her as he spread her legs wide so she was exposed in the most intimate way possible. There was no unease, no shame. Not with the utter reverence in his gaze. With the worship.

His rough fingertips trailed the skin of her inner thighs, eyes on hers.

"Sophie," he growled.

And she knew he was going to demand her to beg again. So she beat him to it.

"Please, Conall," she rasped.

She'd expected to feel shame at being so stripped down to her base needs. To beg a man.

But she wasn't begging a man.

She was begging a *wolf*.

And the wolf ate her up.

And she enjoyed every second of it, her screams music in the midnight air.

※

"Isla, if something happens to me—"

"Ugh, please don't be as cliché as to give me a verbal love letter to regurgitate to the wolf in the event of your untimely death," she said, following Sophie's eyes to Conall, who was sitting in the corner, going over the plan with Thorne and not looking happy about it at all.

Then again, he hadn't been happy since she met him, so this wasn't exactly a change.

And he'd been in a permanent state of fury since they'd only just gotten back from their sexfest in the woods to find Duncan lingering at her front door to tell her it was "witch hunting season."

Obviously Conall had taken that the wrong way, and a growling wolf had threatened to tear at a hulking Scottish vampire.

"*Chill, laddie,*" *Duncan said with a grin. He nodded to Sophie.* "*She's a protected species.*" He clapped Conall on the shoulder, unaware—or maybe cheekily aware—of the fact that Conall was seconds away from ripping his throat out. "*You're part of the gang now. You're gonna have to establish a little thing called a sense of humor so you don't fall on the wrong side of my fangs.*" The threat rolled off his brogue with ease and sincerity.

He stepped back. "All right, let's be off."

And then they were off.

Without even the opportunity to discuss the whole kidnapping thing and plan the murders of the wolves who did it.

Sophie snapped her gaze back to Isla's emerald irises.

"I'd literally have to cut out my own tongue so I had an excuse not to do that and not seem like an asshole for not carrying on my bestie's death wishes," Isla continued. "And I'd have to do it, like a lot, since it would keep growing back. And I like doing stuff with my tongue."

Her eyes cut in the same direction as before, but instead of focusing on her wolf, they locked with Thorne's electric gray irises, which cut to Isla at least every five seconds. Since they'd made up, he didn't seem to want to have her out of the range of his soulful gaze. Isla sighed and looked back to Sophie lazily before sharpening her stare.

"Did you even think of that, Sophie? Of what your death and the wishes following it would do to me, my tongue and, by extension, my sex life?" She pursed her lips. "No, you didn't. You were only thinking of yourself." Isla sipped her wine. "So the only solution to this problem is not to die. It'd piss me right off."

Sophie grinned. That was Isla's way of saying she was worried about her. Her drooling at her aptly droolworthy slayer was as close as she'd get to affection—in public, at least. And Sophie wasn't talking about sex; the vampire had had sex in public a number of times.

She was talking about the kind of love that Sophie had thought was the only myth left in the supernatural world. The kind you died for. More importantly, the kind you lived for.

And Isla had it.

It had changed her, though not much because Isla would rather die than change. She was an ultimate narcissist, loved herself just the way she was. And rightly so. Everyone expected Sophie to grow up just because she was almost two hundred years old. Sophie always cursed those people.

Usually to go gray and wrinkly, because they were so obsessed with maturity.

But Isla had changed as much as she could, and before Thorne, Sophie would've said not one inch. But now, it was enough.

And Sophie liked that for her vampy bestie.

"Isla," Sophie said, sipping her own wine. "I'm serious. There's a high chance we could die on this mission."

Sophie rolled her eyes. "There's a high chance that my immortal brain cells might burst if I continually watch *The Real Housewives of Beverly Hills*," she retorted. "Do I still watch it on the reg? Of course I fucking do, because I love Lisa Rinna."

Sophie grinned again. "Well, this isn't as serious as *Real Housewives*, but I'm going to have to insist that you tell him...." Sophie trailed off, searching for whatever words would even fit inside one sentence. Which would be Isla's limit if she even agreed to do this.

Even if she had a fucking novel, she couldn't say the right words.

Because she didn't know them. The most important thing about growing and controlling powers as a witch was the ability to know oneself. Sophie was seriously sucking at that. Maybe that was why she was like a kid with an industrial-sized fire hose every time she tried to turn on her powers.

Because she was so fucking mixed up that she didn't even know where she ended and the wolf began.

"What? Remind him of a vet appointment?" Isla prompted.

"Just... I don't know. Tell him I didn't hate him," Sophie snapped, draining her wine.

Isla smirked into her own glass. "Is that Shakespeare?"

Sophie poked her tongue out at her. "Forget it. I'll just have to make sure I don't die."

Isla nodded. "Better idea."

❦

THEY STOOD at the back of an unyielding stone building, the air cold, the bite of a Russian winter enough to suck the marrow from your bones.

But the energy of the house was colder still. Evil lived there. Seeped into the very soil the house was built on. Sophie knew that even if it had been the height of summer, she would not have seen a flower. Not a single one.

This was a place even nature knew not to fuck with.

So naturally, Sophie was there.

"Of *course* this is Isla's childhood home," she muttered, stamping her combat boots on the snow for something to do rather than for warmth. She'd already cast a spell over herself to keep her body temp up so she didn't have to dress for the weather.

She despised that.

So she was wearing skintight leather pants that fit her like a glove, and more importantly were easier to get bloodstains out of. She had a low-slung gold looped belt with a moon hanging off one end—it could be used to choke someone with if she was in a pinch, and she really hoped she would be. She hadn't realized how utterly sappy it was until Conall had fingered it in his large hands like it was some precious brand or something.

No thanks.

She was wearing a sheer mesh black long-sleeved top, fingerless leather gloves that went up to her elbows, and a leopard bra peeking through the sheer fabric of her top.

Conall had not been impressed.

"We're going to battle," he gritted out after she'd burned his hand for trying to command her to change.

"And who says a girl can't look good while she does it? Have you even *seen* Daenerys Targaryen?" Sophie replied.

Obviously there'd been an argument. Clearly Sophie had won. Imagine your kind-of werewolf boyfriend trying to tell you what to wear to a face-off with the most evil witch walking?

Honestly, men these days.

"Here," he grunted, holding his hand out to give her something, eyes on the imposing mansion in front of them.

She immediately took it, because it was in her nature to take things when given, no questions asked. It had not worked in her favor in the past when she'd snatched a hand grenade with the pin removed.

Isla thought it was hilarious.

The weight of the gun was cold and foreboding in her hands. She frowned at it, thrusting it at Conall. "I don't want that," she hissed in disgust.

He calmly aimed the barrel downward, away from his chest where she'd been pointing it. "Don't care if you want it."

His hands were tight around the handle—was that what it was called?—so she couldn't let go.

She gave him a look. "You do know the second you let my hand go, I'm just going to hurl it into the snow, right?"

He gave her a hard look. "Then I won't let your hand go."

She scowled. "We can't very well go into battle *holding hands*," she spat. "It's so unprofessional. And gross."

"I won't be holding your hand. I'll be holding a gun, which just happens to be in your hand," he replied.

Sophie's scowl deepened. "I liked you better when you were

mute," she lied. She'd loved the fact he talked more in the short time since she'd saved him from being tortured in a cave in the middle of the woods. It had been a real turning point in the relationship.

He sometimes said words that consisted of more than two syllables. Granted, they'd barely gotten back from their little jaunt in the woods before they'd had to man the battle stations, so they hadn't been able to talk about anything pertaining to their relationship. But they'd argued a lot. He tried to tell her what to do, and she told him she'd turn him into a toad if he tried to stop her from doing what she wanted—like go on quests to kill evil witches.

Just normal couple stuff, Sophie assumed.

His hand flexed around hers, heating it better than any spell. He was only wearing a tee and a light leather jacket, plus his signature jeans and boots combo. His metabolism was crazy high—to the point where Sophie wanted to be a werewolf just so she could consume the sheer amount of calories he did without gaining a pound—so he ran superhot.

And he also was superhot.

But that was neither here nor there.

"I'm not having you go in there without a weapon," he said firmly.

She rolled her eyes. "Um, didn't you get the memo? I *am* the weapon."

His free hand clutched the nape of her neck. "You fight well, babe. You have power unlike anything I have ever seen."

Sophie grinned at the compliment.

He tightened his hold. "But you still bleed." His eyes held demons that couldn't be explained on the eve of battle, only seen. "And anything that bleeds can be lost. I'm not losing you," he promised, either to Sophie or himself, she wasn't sure.

She swallowed a thick and sharp rock at the emotion in his tone and the sudden realization that this battle could have death on its heels. Not hers—she didn't worry about that, since death was always at her heels. No, Conall's. He was the strongest man, and immortal, she'd ever known.

It was always the strongest of men who perished in battles.

Cowards had the pesky habit of surviving.

Not that she was a coward.

And not that she would even entertain the idea of having to face his death. Her own? Sure, why not?

His?

No way in heaven.

She painted on a jaunty smile that she didn't even pull off. "I'll make sure I don't skin my knees, then, shall I?" she said, voice light. Then she used a spell to dissolve the gun in their hands to dust.

She didn't give Conall time to shout at her, or worse, say anything more soulful and intense. She pushed forward.

To battle.

To death.

Whichever came last.

THEY ENTERED through the back door.

Which wasn't locked.

Of course it wasn't locked. You'd have to be mad to break into the house that had everything but a neon sign on top of it reading 'Evil inside, will torture anyone who enters.'

Plus every resident of the town who lived in the perpetual shadow of evil—like Gondor in *Lord of the Rings*—knew exactly what resided in the Mansion of Death, as Sophie had named it.

Secrecy was the biggest rule in the whole of the supernatural community, but they were in the Old Country now, and these mortals knew better than to be calling *Time* magazine. They did everything they could just to survive, just to endure. Plus, they were the people in the world at the least risk of being drained by a vampire. The Rominskitoffs didn't murder in their backyard, apparently.

Sophie and Conall had driven through the town soaked in misery. Well, *Conall* drove. Of course, she, a *woman*, couldn't possibly drive a car in a foreign land. She'd only rescued him from a cage in the middle of the woods where he'd been tortured and then fucked up three fully turned werewolves.

Honestly.

But she wasn't in the mood to argue, because she was psyching herself up for the battle with the binding potion in her hand, and memorizing the spell. She had the power to cast it—which usually required an entire coven of witches—thanks in part to Conall.

Whatever it was between them was something more than sex—even Sophie was beginning to admit that. Because every time they were close, every time they were joined, it was a straight shot of pure power. Like she was a succubus. Except he wasn't drained afterward. If anything, the wolf had more power, more rippling muscles, more of an indestructible aura, the beast in him stronger than ever.

So they'd fucked three times on the jet on the way there—strictly for battle purposes—then twice on the train from Poland.

She was more juiced than a guido in June.

"Don't you think it's weird that the vamps have a kitchen when they don't even need to eat?" Sophie asked conversationally as Conall ripped the throat of a vampire guard who'd rushed them upon entering the vast room.

He'd been snacking on the cook, who scuttled out silently. Humans who didn't scream at death were troubling, because that meant they'd seen worse things than death.

Join the club.

"Like, I know vampires can eat. Have you seen Isla eat a

cheeseburger?" She shook her head. "I swear she does it to taunt me because she can't put on weight, the bitch." Worry for her vamp saturated the insult. Isla was currently in the front of the house, facing off with her mother and brothers. Sure, she had Duncan and her possessive slayer with her, who wouldn't let her die out of sheer force of will and large biceps, but still, dread had set over Sophie the second they'd set foot inside.

She stuck to her nonchalance, trailing her hand over the stainless-steel surface, finding modern amenities in the ancient house strange. "I know they'd likely eat too, but I thought it'd be unicorn hearts, newborn babies, that kind of thing."

Sophie glanced at Conall, who'd dropped the headless vamp and was inhaling deeply, looking for the scent of an enemy.

His eyes flared in panic and he moved toward her. The vampire had already dropped to the floor without Sophie having to take her eyes off Conall. "Gotta be quicker than that, wolf," she teased, stepping over the vamp toward where the witch was being held.

She didn't need a map of Castle Douche-ala to know where she was. No, even with the sheer evil that soaked the walls of the house—that was in the very air she breathed here—there was malice so cold that it worked like a magnet, drawing Sophie in.

The way was relatively unguarded, Conall taking care of the rest because he'd growled at her to "conserve your power" when she'd decapitated the third vamp with a flip of her hands.

Sophie had rolled her eyes, mostly because he was right.

She might've had more power flowing through her veins than ever before, but that likely might not be enough. She didn't trust herself to call on the power inside of her, so much so that she'd done a small binding spell on herself. Silly, on the eve of battle, but even with the spell, something about the dark witch's call was alluring to that caged part of her. It rattled against her interior walls, not to destroy the ancient witch but join her.

Not good, like *at all*.

She froze when she found herself standing at the top of a flight of stairs. The damp air was drenched in death, and black magic so wrong that it turned her stomach.

Conall's heat kissed her back, and he rested his hands lightly on her hips. The small touch soothed Sophie, as much as she hated to admit it.

"*La mia luna?*" he rasped, voice drenched in worry.

She sucked in a breath. It was tainted with the bitter magic, seeping into Sophie's lungs painfully. "I'm good," she said. "Let's rock out with our magicks out."

Then she descended.

༄

THERE WAS NOT A SINGLE SOUL, or vampire, guarding the witch. Sophie guessed why. Walking through the dungeons was harder and harder the closer they got. As if the air was getting thicker, turning to cement. The very oxygen surrounding the witch repelled life.

The power inside of Sophie clawed at her painfully, so bad in fact that she had to sink her teeth into the side of her lip in order to stop herself from crying out. She knew if Conall so much as sensed that she was in any kind of pain, he'd throw her over his shoulder and sprint out of the house quicker than she could blink.

He didn't care about the end of the world that may come as he did so.

He'd said as much on the plane.

"I'm going to be in danger here," Sophie said throatily, tucked in his arms, naked on the sofa of her private jet. *That's why she didn't fly commercial—you couldn't fuck in the middle of the cabin. Well, you could, but people frowned upon it.*

"I'll likely even get hurt," she continued. *Conall's arms flexed. She rested her elbow on his chest so she could hold her chin in her hand and lock eyes*

with him. "You're gonna wanna go all wolfy and protect me and pound on your chest, prove to everyone you can look after your woman." She gave him a look. "But in there, I'm not going to be your woman. I'm your witch—actually, I'm always your witch—the one who has kickass powers and also a responsibility to take in a power that threatens to burn the world to the ground. You gotta stand aside and let me get a little banged up, for the greater good. I know, it's totally lame. I'd rather do it for the greater evil, but someone already stole that part."

Conall stared at her, his eyes warming the chill of what was to come. Then he wrenched her up his body so their foreheads were almost touching. His hands clutched the sides of her neck.

"I'm never going to stand aside," he growled. "I'll be at your side, fighting for you when I can, fighting with you when I can't." He searched her face. "I'd set fire to the world just to stop you from feeling a cold breeze, so don't think I'm going to care about someone else burning it down if it means I take you from harm's way."

She blinked. Once. Twice. His certainty, his determination, surrounded her. Enchanted her.

The memories of his howl, his sorrow, not yet to come haunted her with a chill that even the burning of the world wouldn't warm.

So instead of replying, she kissed him. Like she might die that day. Even though she knew she wouldn't. But she would die soon. And she'd be taking two people to the grave with her.

The memory fueled her. Both of his touch before and of what was going to come of this entire war: her death, his pain. She needed to punish those responsible while she could. Before it was too late.

The witch was standing in the middle of a dim chamber, eyes on Sophie the second she rounded the corner, as if she had been waiting for her. She smiled when their eyes met, showing blackened, decaying teeth. A centipede scuttled from the inside of her mouth, up her cheek and into her hair.

Sophie didn't blanche, but she felt the wolf behind her stutter in his step. He shouldn't have even made it that far. The magic in the dungeon should've brought him to his knees. There was a spell in play there that allowed only those with magic—dark magic—to enter. Sophie didn't want to dwell too hard on the reason she got through it, let alone him.

She used their slight distance to throw the two crystals she'd been clutching at the arched entrance to the antechamber, the one she was inside of and he was outside of. They landed at each end, erecting an invisible but impenetrable wall between them. She'd planned on that all along, never intending to put her wolf in the line of fire.

She knew he wouldn't die that day, but there were a lot of things worse than death. She was already responsible for what befell him in the future; she wouldn't be letting anything happen to him in the present.

The betrayal and rage in his eyes as soon as he realized what she'd done hit her physically. He pounded against the wall, screaming, bellowing, his form changing as he prepared to turn into a wolf in an effort to charge through the magic.

Sophie turned, not revealing an ounce of emotion.

She faced the witch, who hadn't even glanced at the wolf. Her gaze was toxic, seeming to rot Sophie's very flesh.

"I have been waiting for you, child." Her voice was nails on a chalkboard, tearing at Sophie's ears.

Hot blood trickled down her earlobes. She knew if she let the witch speak for too much longer, there'd be more blood. Her very words were drenched in evil so deep that it tore at Sophie's insides.

The pain was more intense than she'd expected. Especially with Conall's frenzied roars at feeling it secondhand, through whatever connection had suddenly grown stronger in proximity to this ancient evil.

"Well, color me flattered. One of the most terrible and, I've got to say, unattractive witches in our race has been waiting for little old me." Sophie clutched the bottle in her hands, though something stopped her from moving, from tossing the potion at the witch.

At first Sophie thought it was the witch, weaving a spell. But no, it was Sophie herself. She didn't *want* to cast the spell. She wanted to hear more. To bathe longer in the acid that was the air around the witch.

The sheer power.

"You have power that surpasses everything," Malena continued, eyes glowing black. "You see a sister in me. You know we will do great things." Her voice was suddenly music.

Sophie stepped forward. Not to bind her, as had been the plan, but to release her. She needed Sophie's help. This great and benevolent being needed Sophie to help release her, to make them pay.

"I see what they have done to you," Malena continued. "They fear your power. So they seek to destroy it. Because they are not like you. You have never had the comfort of a sister because you are too strong for them. And you sought only freedom. They offer you a cage to whither and die in. I offer death too. You know this. Death is your very existence." Her eyes glowed brighter and darker at the same time with the knowledge of Sophie's secret.

It was a weight being lifted off her, that someone else knew. That someone else understood what it was to manipulate death, to be borne out of it.

Sophie took another step forward. More blood streamed from her ears, warm on her neck.

"But with this death I offer life. I offer *power*."

The invitation was inches away. Sophie needed to take one more step to grasp it. Her skin started to blister at her hands. That didn't matter.

Worms curled around her feet. Large spiders crawled up her legs.

She was about to take the last step when the entire room vibrated.

"Sophie!" The growl was a bellow louder than the roar of power around them. It was familiar, full of something warm, something that melted the ice surrounding her.

She glanced back, her eyes tearing from the orbs of destruction attached to the witch's head. Her gaze met gold.

Conall stood stationary against Sophie's wall of magic. His clothes were ripped, knuckles bloody. "You shall not do this," he rasped. "Or the world will burn. With me inside it."

"No!" Malena hissed, sensing the wolf's pull was stronger than even her own magic.

But it was too late. Sophie had already thrown the potion, watched it smash at Malena's feet, all the power that had been peeling at Sophie's soul sucked into the void created by her potion.

She held up a black stone and every part of Malena's control and black magic tore into it, cracking the bones in Sophie's hand. Still she held strong, gritting her teeth.

"From the abomination of our gift, let the release of your powers be swift. Let this darkness be home to your power, for you lose it now, in this moment, in this hour," Sophie chanted, her voice scratching with the pain it took to say the words. The witch had tried to fight against it, tried to yank Sophie's voice from inside her.

Though she'd failed. And now Sophie held her darkness in the pulsating stone. It burned her skin and froze it, her broken bones protesting.

It wouldn't hold forever. Or for very long. But it worked for now.

Sophie released the spell keeping Conall out. He burst into the room with a rush of warmth, of energy.

Sophie sank to her knees, unable to stand with her pain any longer.

Conall's hands were at her arms in an instant, to yank her back up, to hold her.

"No," she hissed, her voice so sharp that it paused even her wolf.

She nodded to Malena, who she was keeping frozen with great effort.

Blood ran from her nose.

"Get the witch," she gritted out.

He paused, and she sensed his pain, his fury at her state. She couldn't move her gaze from the murderous glare of Malena. "Do it!" she screamed, power vibrating in her voice.

Conall moved, yanking at the witch roughly, snapping her wrist as he did so.

No love lost there.

His gaze was on Sophie, who was still on the ground.

"I will carry you both," he said, stepping forward and dragging the witch.

"No," Sophie whispered, pushing her screaming body up with a force that roiled her stomach.

Conall's eyes flickered from gold to silver as his beast sensed her pain, her danger.

"Let's go. This place is tired, don't you think?" she asked lightly.

He growled in response. "Sophie, you cannot walk out of here."

She spat blood at his feet, turning as she did so. "Oh, I can, and I'll be doing it with all of my usual swagger. Just you watch."

And she did.

And it almost killed her.

But it wasn't her day to die.

So she did it.

Chapter Ten

"I'm sure it doesn't measure up to a cave, but here's a little hovel I prepared earlier," Sophie said with a forced grin, holding her hand out to the cage she'd replaced on the off chance she'd need it to hold any rogue vampire-human hybrids.

Luckily, with some tweaking, it served as a multipurpose prison, suitable to hold a witch who some of the most powerful immortals in the world had to put in a cave on a cliff in Albania thousands of years before.

This was in Sophie's offices in Brooklyn. Close enough.

The witch snarled, and the stone tucked between Sophie's breasts on a thick chain throbbed with a force that cracked a rib.

She was starting to feel like Frodo heaving that fucking ring into Mount Doom.

Conall shoved the witch with a brutal force that sent her flying into the metal of the cage, which shocked her on contact. His face curled into a grim sort of satisfaction.

Then he turned to Sophie, body taut and wired, as it had been since they'd left Isla's home.

They had met up with a bloodied and frantic Thorne cradling a lifeless Isla in his arms. Sophie noted the unnatural angle of her neck and reasoned that she'd had it broken, hence the reason for her being unconscious. A wound like that could take them out of commission for a hot minute, but it was no biggie.

"Ah, looks like you've got what we came for," Duncan boomed, an edge to his forced cheerful voice that turned Sophie's stomach once more. He craned his head to get a look at the being Conall had been carrying with disgust. "Ah, she's a looker, isn't she? The evilest ones always are." He winked at the witch.

Sophie blinked, her head pounding with the need for unconsciousness as she followed Duncan's gaze in confusion. Malena's face was curled in a grimace, her lips black with crusted bits of dead meat from what Sophie assumed was her last meal. Her eyes were black, completely, even without her power inside her. Her hair was matted and rank with insects crawling through it. The dress she wore was so ripped it barely covered her decaying frame, and it had a rancid stench attached to it.

Sophie had assumed that Conall could see what she saw, hence the reason for his utter abhorrence for touching her.

But no, she must've had a strong glamour that only witches could see through.

Her wolf's disgust was purely from the fact that the witch had almost killed his mate.

Ah, not yet, wolf, *she thought*. But soon.

She swayed slightly and Conall let out a growl, dropping the witch as if she were nothing but a sack of potatoes so he could steady Sophie.

"How about we don't drop the all-evil being who we almost paid our lives for retrieving," Sophie said through gritted teeth.

"Already on it," Duncan replied with a grin, heaving the witch over his shoulder, smacking at her ass while he did so.

Sophie toyed with the idea of taking the glamour off so he could see the rotting corpse he was fondling, but thought better of it. This was more fun, and she was in dire need of amusement.

"La mia luna," Conall murmured, his hands biting into her hips.

"I'm good. Don't you dare try to carry me," she snapped.

"If you haven't noticed, Isla is fucking dead right now, and we're exposed," Thorne thundered, entering the conversation finally. He glared at her wolf. "Pick her the fuck up, knock her out if you need to, and let's get out of here so Sophie can fucking heal her," he growled.

Sophie sensed Conall might challenge Thorne, but the slayer was already jogging down the snowy incline, toward their vehicles, his concern for Isla his only worry.

Well, that sounded familiar.

"Wolf," she warned. But she was already in his arms.

Fucking alpha males.

They'd rushed to the airport, taken off and flown for an hour without Isla waking up. Even though Sophie was distracted trying to contain the epitome of all evil, battling unconsciousness, she was a smidge worried.

But of course, Isla had to wake up with style. And totally steal her thunder on binding the witch single-handedly by letting the cabin know her human husband who her family had killed—and who had her 'Jack the Ripper' an entire continent for fifty years—was actually alive, a vampire, and the head of the rebellion. Along with her mother.

"IF SOMEONE DOESN'T MAKE a movie out of my life, I'm going to be so totally pissed off," she'd said in the car from the airport. "That means all of it would've been for nothing." Thorne gave her a pointed look. "What?" she asked with faux innocence. "I'm sorry. You're okay and all, but seeing my brilliance on the silver screen? Doesn't compare."

They'd stopped at Sophie's offices.

Isla eyed the witch. "You've got this from here, right?" she asked. "I don't mean like forever, I mean just like locking her up while we go figure out what the fuck to do with her. You've got your doggy bodyguard slash luggage assistant. Luggage being one crazy evil witch." She winked. "Make sure you tip him well."

Sophie had told her bestie "we got this" even though she'd been vaguely *worried that, for once in her life, she didn't 'got this', because she saw that the thread Isla had been holding onto for five hundred years was about to snap with the news of Jonathan.*

His death had followed her through the ages and was a small contributing factor to why she was fucked up. The rest of it was just because she was a narcissistic bitch. A fun one, though.

The clang of the cage hurtled Sophie back to the present. Her mind was getting whiplash from all the back and forth.

Conall clutched the sides of her head, his face tight with worry. He seemed to sense she was about to lose it.

"She gonna be able to get outta here anytime soon?" he clipped, jerking his head toward the cage.

"No," Sophie said confidently. Her spell on the cage was fucking fantastic. It'd hold for the time being. Not forever, because eventually the binding spell would wear off and the crystal around her neck would return power to its rightful owner. If they hadn't figured something out by then, they were fucked.

She was in his arms and halfway down the stairs before she knew what was going on.

"What are you—" she started to protest. But the security and warmth of Conall's arms was what finally let her bruised and battered mind succumb to the abyss.

⁂

HE PACED the area in front of the bed, about to rip the skin from his bones.

Sophie was still. So still he had to check her heartbeat every five seconds to make sure she wasn't dead. But he'd know if she was dead.

He'd be in insurmountable pain. If his mate had left this world, then he wouldn't be thinking about ripping the skin from his bones—he'd be doing it already.

But death clung to her from her time with that monster. He could sense it. He could fucking *taste* it, like acid on his tongue.

Never in his life had he been scared. Of anything. He had been through pain, suffering, the loss of his entire family, betrayal of his clan, torture, the solitude of the moon that killed most wolves.

But never fear.

The moments Sophie was in that antechamber, with that... *thing* and he was helpless to do a fucking thing, had been the most terrifying of his entire existence.

Worse, because he could see that Sophie—or the darkness within her—almost crossed over to a place that he would never get her back from. The rankest of evils, that charred and chewed souls so bad that even Hades wouldn't take them.

If she had, he would've followed her without question. At least his charred soul would have her blackened one. He was not afraid of his own damnation.

It was hers that boiled his blood.

He also sensed the weakness creeping at her, the power yanking at every available source the entire time she battled to keep the witch contained. It had almost killed her.

And he'd been fucking *powerless*.

He was going to do anything in his power to get this evil ended, the one outside her and the one within her. He was going to do everything outside of his power too. Because humans in love did impossible things to save their soul mates. Wolves would do so much more. This wolf would do *everything*.

He'd burn this fucking world to the ground.

He was a king, by birth and by blood. He was never going to be powerless. He'd take back his throne, have his mate—his witch *queen*—at his side, and he'd watch the fucking world burn.

Acknowledgments

I am lucky enough to have some amazing people in my life who encourage me and put up with my crazy when I'm writing. And my crazy when I'm not writing too.

Mum. You've always been my biggest cheerleader, my best friend and my sometimes therapist. If it wasn't for you, I wouldn't know the magic of reading and I wouldn't be able to write a word. Thank you for telling me I could be anything I wanted to be. I'd never be who I am today if it wasn't for you.

My **Dad.** You're not here with us but you're the reason why I can shoot a gun, ride a motorbike, shop like a champ, and believe in myself. I miss you every day.

Michelle and **Caro**. You two ladies are so very special and your generosity and support is amazing. I'm so lucky I have you.

Jessica Gadziala. My #sisterqueen. You've cheered me on when I didn't believe in myself and given me a friendship that is all about straightening crowns.

This book wouldn't be what it is without my wonderful team of betas. These special ladies helped to make this book what it is.

Ginny, Amy, Sarah, and **Annette** you are wonderful.

Harriet, Polly and Emma. My girls. The ones who talk me down when I'm getting crazy, or bring a bottle of wine and get crazy with me. True friendships are rare in this world, but I've got it with you ladies.

And to **you, the reader**. Thank you. Thank you for reading my books. Thank you for taking a chance on something different from me. Thanks for every e-mail, comment, and review you give me. I treasure each and every one.

About the Author

Anne Malcom has been an avid reader since before she can remember, her mother responsible for her book addiction. It started with magical journeys into the world of Hogwarts and Middle Earth, then as she grew up her reading tastes grew with her. Her obsession with books and romance novels in particular gave Anne the opportunity to find another passion, writing. Finding writing about alpha males and happily ever afters more fun than reading about them, Anne is not about to stop any time soon.

Raised in small town New Zealand, Anne had a truly special childhood, growing up in one of the most beautiful countries in the world. She has backpacked across Europe, ridden camels in the Sahara, eaten her way through Italy, and had all sorts of crazy adventures. For now, she's back at home in New Zealand and quite happy. But who knows when the travel bug will bite her again.

Want to get stalking?
Check out Anne's website
Email her at: annemalcomauthor@hotmail.com
Join her amazing reader group

Also by Anne Malcom

The Vein Chronicles

Fatal Harmony

Deathless

Eternity's Awakening — *Coming Soon*

The Sons of Templar MC

Making the Cut

Firestorm

Outside the Lines: A Sons of Templar Novella

Out of the Ashes

Beyond the Horizon

Dauntless

Unquiet Mind

Echoes of Silence

Skeletons of Us

Broken Shelves

Greenstone Security

Still Waters

Shield

> # Standalones

Birds of Paradise

Made in the USA
Middletown, DE
17 April 2022